LEE HOLLAND

A CHAIR IN TIME

A PLAYDATE WITH HISTORY

ISBN: 979-8-88945-321-5

eISBN: 979-8-88945-322-2

Brilliant Books Literary

137 Forest Park Lane Thomasville

North Carolina 27360 USA

Printed in the United States of America

FOREWORD

This book is a natural link of a man who is a history major and a proud grandpa with a vivid imagination; and what a wonderful result... an entertaining story that everyone can relate to, with actual history added for good measure. Textbook publishers and school districts could learn a thing or two from this genre.

In the previous book, *Welcome to My Chair: Tales of Adventure From Grumpy's Living Room*, we met Grumpy who took his granddaughters, Sarah and Hannah, on amazing adventures all from the comfort of his old, worn out recliner. In this book, Grammy and Grumpy have passed away, and the girls have inherited more than just the broken down chair. They have gained the ability to open worlds with their imagination as well as a love of history. They explore the past and bond as only siblings can. Grumpy's undying sense of adventure runs through the girls' veins to their very core.

The first time I read a portion of this book to my family, we laughed about the realistic interaction between the girls in the story, with a large part including arguing.

After reading half way through the chapter, I heard an enthusiastic, "That's right! Sarah does always get her way. I never do." I continued reading to be interrupted again with, "Hannah does do stuff just like that, just to annoy me... all the time!" Before we knew what happened, we had squabbling in stereo; my reading of the story with the echo of real bickering inspired by the story. We had to pause and just laugh because every parent and every sibling has had the same disagreements with the same sense of injustice. Anyone with a brother or sister will reminisce about growing up as they read the following pages, both older siblings who had more responsibility and more privileges as well as younger siblings who had the advantage of getting away with more stuff because they were the "baby."

You now have the opportunity to enjoy the journey of two young sisters as they experience different worlds and different times. You have a book that will make you laugh and appreciate history and hopefully life. As for me, I've gotten to see my daughters' wealth of experiences expand exponentially, and I undoubtedly will have that old, broken down, thread bare chair that won't match anything at my house before all is said and done. Know that you are getting off pretty well in the deal. I hope you enjoy the book *A Chair in Time: a Playdate with History.*

Amber Bryant

They took home the chair and helped it survive,
The two little girls enabled the magic to revive.
Time travel is possible, you can depend on that,
A playdate with history from wherever the chair sat.

A horn, some goggles, and a red hard hat,
They added a little of this and some of that.
A trip back in history and what do they see?
A train, a steamship, and an Indian or three.

Adventurers, some soldiers, and a horse-drawn coach,
Trouble getting home but they never gave up hope.
They squabbled, they fussed on their trip back in time,
Regardless of what happened, they came home every time.

A CHAIR IN TIME

*T**ime Travel.* Is it possible? Does anyone really *want* to travel in time? *Should* anyone travel in time? What would it take to travel back in time? What would be seen? What would be heard? Who would be seen? How would they communicate? How would they get back home?

Keep reading and you will find out. Time travel is possible. Just ask a couple of sisters who built such a machine and went back in time on many different occasions and added many new experiences to their adventures. It was all made possible by a big, ugly, worn-out chair that had taken them on many magical adventures with their grandfather, Grumpy. So put a smile on your face, a little magic in your heart, and enjoy only what children are capable of doing. Join the girls as they take a journey in time and visit actual places and events in our history. The excursion will be well worth your time.

CHAPTER ONE

This book is about the adventures of two sisters, Sarah and Hannah. The old chair had taken them on so many adventures with their grandfather when they were preschoolers. When their grandparents had gone on their final solo adventures, the girls just had to have the chair. They persuaded their parents, over many loud and determined protests, to take it home with them. The chair was placed in the living room, even though it looked a little out of place amongst all the other furniture. But out of place or not, the girls enjoyed the chair, and it reminded them of the many magical adventures that they had experienced with their Grumpy. The chair still smelled as it had when he used to sit in it. To their eyes, the chair was not worn-out or lumpy; it was still a wonderful chair that they could just sit in and reminisce about the past. They often contentedly recalled all the good things that had occurred in the chair with their loving grandfather.

As comforting and enjoyable as the old chair was to the girls, it just wasn't quite the same. Sure they still had adventures and exploits. But it was not the same as it had once been when the chair was at Grumpy's house. There he had participated in the forays into magical realms. One day, Sarah, the older of the two girls, decided it was time to liven up that old chair. It was time to recreate the magic that Grumpy had been able to elicit from the recliner. Taking her little sister, Hannah, into her confidence, the two made plans. They developed a list of all the required items that would be needed to "improve" the chair. The girls asked their mother to take them to their grandparent's house before it was finally cleaned up and ready to be put up for sale. They needed to get some things from the garage.

The girl's mother, Amber, asked, "Why do you want to go to Grammy's house? What could you possibly need to get from that junky old garage?"

Sarah just smiled and said, "It's a secret. But it will be lots of fun."

So with their mother shaking her head, they loaded themselves into the car and drove the short distance to Grumpy's house. Most people opening the garage door would be amazed and a little frightened to see such a "junkified" mess before their eyes. The garage contained the collection of almost fifty years of marriage, over forty years of construction equipment, thirty years of teaching paraphernalia as well as twenty-five-plus years of children's "stuff." The garage was a mess. Grumpy would tell anyone daring to venture out into the garage that there was a map and a shotgun by the door. A sign above the garage door said "Enter at Your Own Risk." He had said that any intrepid travelers would be on their own wiles for at least three days. After three days, Grumpy would send out a search and rescue party. So far, no daring adventurers had ever been lost for more than a few days in the garage. Grumpy always said, "If we ever had anything in this marriage, we still have it."

Well the girls were undaunted, at least as long as there was an adult present to give them some reassurance and moral support. Entering the garage, Sarah's eyes took in all the items that had once belonged to Grammy and Grumpy, and she remembered all the good times she had with her grandparents. She wished her Grumpy could join them on this new quest. He would have been the first one to sign on to undertake such a pursuit. Grumpy would be sadly missed! He had always been happy to take part in any of the girl's adventures.

After standing there for a few moments, Sarah took out their list, and she and Hannah began scouring the garage for the necessary items. This was a monumental undertaking because of the magnitude of the accumulation of all different types of interesting items. Some of the things that were gathered up were a wind-up alarm clock, an old rotary phone, and an old computer keyboard with cord still attached. Additional items included a roll of duct tape, ball of twine, some goggles, and a set of headphones, and not to be forgotten was an old blue-and-white record player. No time machine would be complete nor any time traveler fully equipped without the ubiquitous record player. She also picked up Grumpy's old cell phone. A time traveler never knows who she might want to call from a long time ago. Hannah stopped and picked up an umbrella. To this, Sarah said, "What's that for? That's not on our list!"

Hannah replied, "Actually, we might need the bumbershoot to keep us dry if we get in the rain."

Sarah said, "Okay, that might not be such a bad idea." Sarah continued to paw around in a box of old military, hiking, and camping equipment. From the box, she collected a couple of canteens, a topographical map, a compass, and Grumpy's hiking stick. Digging farther into the box, she found Grumpy's old tanker helmet complete with microphone and cord still attached.

As they were leaving the garage, Hannah spotted another box of "stuff." Stopping to investigate, she dug around in the box and found a bicycle horn. She tucked it under one arm and continued to rummage in the box. In the box, she also found a construction hard hat, a pair of welder's goggles, some leather gloves, and the ever-popular pocket calculator. How could they survive in the past without a calculator? Digging a little deeper, she found a clipboard with a pencil attached by a small chain.

Dumping all the paraphernalia into the back of the car, the girls said they we ready to go. After climbing in themselves, they made the trip home. As the equipment was being unloaded from the car, their mother asked the kids what they were going to do with all that junk. To this Sarah and Hannah replied, "It's a surprise! It will be a lot of fun. We're going on an adventure!" As they carried the junk into the house, the girls piled it all on the chair or on the floor beside it.

"This is going to be so much fun!" Hannah said. "Let's get started."

About that time, Mom entered the room and saw all the contents of Grumpy's garage piled in her living room. She told the girls, "Having that old chair in the house is bad enough, but all the stuff on the chair is not going to stay. Take it to your room. It will not stay in the living room. Now go!"

To this the girls cried, "But, Mom!"

"But me no buts! Take all that junk to your room."

As the girls began to gather up the contents from Grumpy's garage, Sarah replied, "But, Mom, we need the chair. All that stuff is needed to make the chair into our time machine. We need the chair!"

Their mother stated, "Not in my living room! Now go! In fact, take all that stuff to the garage!"

Hannah and Sarah looked at each other, smiled, and began to carry all the important "junk" out to the garage. Soon everything was cleaned up. They then went to their mother and asked for help to move the chair out to the garage. They would need help because the chair was much too large for the girls to move by themselves. So the three of them grabbed hold of the chair, the two girls on the front and their mother at the back. After a little straining and with only a few scrapes of the chair against the wall, it was located in an out-of-the-way spot in the garage. The chair had found a new home. The chair was happy. The girls were happy because now they could begin their adventure, and Mom was happy because that old, ugly, worn-out chair was no longer in the living room. Everybody was happy.

CHAPTER TWO

With the chair and the accouterments assembled, all was right with the world and the transformation commenced. The one-car space in the two-car garage was now filled with the chair and the required items that would become a time machine. The two girls began at once the makeover of the chair.

Sarah began the chair conversion by selecting the alarm clock. "This alarm clock will be what controls if we go forward or back in time. We can put it here," said Sarah, as she opened the large padded arm of the chair. A large opening in the arm of the chair was revealed. The arms extended out from the chair at right angles. Sarah announced, "Look! The chair now has wings. That will help us fly." Putting the clock next to her ear, she listened to make sure it was ticking before she stuffed it into the opening.

Next, she picked up the computer and said, "To go back in time, all we have to do is punch the date on the keyboard and that will be the time we can go back to. We will have to connect the computer to the clock or we might go in the wrong direction. Hannah, give me the twine."

Hannah handed her the compass. At this, Sarah said, "Not the compass. The twine!"

"I don't know what 'twine' is!" responded Hannah.

"Twine looks like small rope. That ball of small rope over there," explained Sarah.

"Oh, that's what that is? I wondered what that was." Handing the twine to Sarah, she said, "Here is the 'small rope.' Now I know what twine is."

"Now, Hannah, hand me the scissors."

"I don't got no scissors," replied Hannah, still clinging to her childish double negatives.

"Hannah! How am I going to cut the twine if I don't have scissors?"

"Chew on it like a mouse," said Hannah as she ran to the kitchen to get Sarah a pair of scissors.

When she returned with the scissors, Sarah had one end fastened around the stem of the alarm clock. Holding the spool of twine in her one hand, she reached for the scissors with the other. Hannah stopped well out of arm's reach from the chair and said, "I want to cut the 'small rope.' You always get to cut everything. It's my turn."

Knowing it was useless to argue, Sarah held out the twine and said, "Okay. Cut it right here. Don't make it too short."

Taking one end of the twine, Sarah tried to attach it to the phone. This proved to be harder than she anticipated. There was no place to fasten the cord. She thought for a moment or two and then asked her sister to pass her the tape. To this, Hannah, staying out of arm's reach, said, "I want to tear the tape. You always get to do it."

"Okay, okay. Tear off a small strip so I can fasten the string to the phone."

Hannah commenced unspooling about two feet of tape. As she attempted to tear the tape, the tape would not cooperate and began to wad up and stick to itself. Before long, she had tape unwound, matted, twisted, stuck to her fingers, and completely discombobulated. In other words, a complete mess!

Sarah took the tape from Hannah and spooled off about a two-inch strip and declared, "Take the scissors and cut the tape right here. Be careful and don't cut my fingers!"

With the right size tape, she fastened the twine to the computer. At about this point, Hannah said, "Sarah, why didn't you use the computer cord to attach it to the clock?"

Sarah pondered this oversight for a moment or two and then said, "Oh. We need that to attach it to the phone."

"What do we need the phone for?"

"That's in case we get lost."

As Sarah finished fastening the phone to the computer keyboard, she looked over, and Hannah was busy taping the bicycle horn to the arm of the chair. Seeing the handiwork, which used up about half the roll of tape, she said, "Hannah! What's that for?"

"That's in case somebody gets in our way. We can honk the horn, and they will get out of our way."

"No. Hannah, there won't be anyone in front of us. We are the first ones. No one has done this before. Besides, the horn can't go there. That's where the record player is going to set."

"But I want to put it here."

"No, Hannah."

"I never get my way. Why do you always get your way?"

Sarah removed the offending item and put the blue-and-white record player in its place. Asking Hannah for the twine and duct tape, she was met with the statement, "I get to cut. You always get to cut. I never get to cut anything." So holding out the cord for Hannah to cut, she then had Hannah cut a piece of tape. After attaching them together, she looked up and saw that Hannah was now fastening the horn to the back of the chair. She told her sister, "No, Hannah. That doesn't go there."

"I never get to do anything!"

"Hannah, that's where we will put the umbrella. That way we won't get wet if it rains. Okay?"

"Oh. That's a good idea." With those words, she began to tape the bumbershoot to the headrest of the chair.

While Hannah was grappling the umbrella into place, Sarah took a little bit of tape and fastened the compass to the record player. She told her sister, "With the compass right here, we will always know what direction we are heading." Finishing her handiwork, she looked up and there was Hannah starting to tape the horn to the telephone. As she removed the horn, she said to her little sis, "It might get in the way if we have to use the phone."

"I never get to do anything I want to do." Hannah pouted.

Sarah responded, "Hannah, hand me the map. We won't know where to go without the map."

Hannah gave her the map, and Sarah folded it and stuffed it into the lid of the record player. The task completed, Sarah exclaimed, "There, now as we steer the time machine we can see where we are going."

"I never get to use my ideas. I have good ideas too," grumbled Hannah.

"We need to hook up the headphones," Sarah said. "Where are your headphones?"

Hannah went to the pile that still remained on the floor and brought over the headphones. She took a bit of tape and some string and fastened one end of the twine to the phone and the other end to the ear piece of the headphone. No sooner had she done that than Sarah took the end of the phone off and taped it to the computer. She explained, "Everything must go through the computer."

"I never get to do what I want," muttered Hannah.

As Hannah was giving her soliloquy, Sarah made her trip to the junk pile and brought back Grumpy's old tanker helmet with the attached cord. Taking some tape, she fastened the cord to the computer. "With this helmet and your earphone, we can talk to each other while we are in the time continuum. Otherwise we would be going faster that the sound of our voices. We would not know what we were saying."

"No! I want Grumpy's helmet! You can use the earphones! You always get to use the good stuff!"

"But, Hannah, I found Grumpy's helmet. Besides I'm older and I'm the leader. I get to wear the helmet." As she said those words, she looked up and there was Hannah busy using the rest of the roll of tape to fasten the bicycle horn to the umbrella handle. Sarah began removing the horn from the umbrella.

"No, Hannah. If you put the horn on there we won't be able to raise and lower the umbrella. We have to be able to lower the umbrella when we travel at light speeds or we might lose it in the vortex of time."

"I don't get to wear the helmet. I don't get to put the horn anyplace on the chair. I don't get to do anything. I have good ideas. We never get to use my ideas. What do I get to do?" whined Hannah.

Sarah thought for a minute. "Go get Grumpy's red hard hat. I've got a great idea."

As Hannah went to the junk pile to find the hard hat, she mumbled the entire time. "I don't get to do what I want. Sarah always gets what she wants. Why does she always get her way? I have good ideas. We never get to use my ideas."

When she found the hat and had brought it back to the chair, Sarah said, "Give me the hat and the horn. I've got a great idea." She took the horn and the hat and then asked for the tape. With a sour look on her face, Hannah handed the duct tape to Sarah. Sarah combined the hat, horn, and tape. When she had completed her task, she handed the creation to her younger sister and said, "See? Now wasn't that a great idea?"

Hannah took one look at the chapeau and the scowl on her face turned into a big grin. Taking the hard hat from her sister, she carefully placed it on her head. The hat was too large and came down over her ears, but it didn't seem to matter. With the ill-fitting hat in place, she reached up and squeezed the end of the horn. *Honk. Honk. Honk. Honk. Honk. Honk. Honk.* The honking was almost as loud as her grin. This was great! Now she could do her time traveling in style. What a great idea! She was glad she thought of it.

While all this honking was taking place, Sarah picked out the pocket calculator and connected it with twine to the computer. "We can use this to figure out how far back in time we actually go. It can also tell us how fast we are going."

Honk. Honk. Honk. Honk. Honk. Honk.

"Hannah! Please stop all that honking. We're not even going anywhere yet. Please stop." With those words, she went into the house and returned a few minutes later with a flashlight. "This is in case it gets dark before we get back." She began taping the flashlight to the chair.

Honk. Honk. Honk. Honk. Honk.

"Hannah, we're almost ready to go back in time. Let's get ready. Okay?"

Honk. Honk. Honk. "Okay. Sure. What do we do?" *Honk. Honk.*

CHAPTER THREE

From the very beginning of this quest, Sarah had taken into account that one can't just get in a purpose-built chair and penetrate the fabric of time itself. Preparing for any contingency that might occur, the sisters went over to the remaining pile of "stuff" and began sorting out the required equipment.

Sarah said, "First, we have to put on our equipment for the trip." So for the next few minutes, between all the honking, the intrepid adventurers suited up in the latest time traveling apparel. There was nine year old Sarah in the new time vortex uniform covering her slender, almost skinny frame. Grumpy's tanker helmet (with microphone) was ensconced on her head and revealed dark blond tendrils of hair curling around the edges of the green helmet. Goggles were covering her pastel blue eyes and a large pair of men's leather gloves with gauntlets protected her hands. At the end of her long legs were flip flops decorated with pink and white flowers. To complete her ensemble, a dashing bright red scarf was stylishly coiled around her slender neck. She cut quite a dashing figure, even if she did say so herself. The grin of her face displayed silver braces that were fighting to close the gap in her front teeth.

Next there was Hannah. Even at five years old she was complete and ultra-chic. Beginning at the top of her of her blond head was the red chapeau with bicycle horn attached by silver duct tape. Earphones with twine connecting it to the computer, a red scarf draped around her neck, large leather work gloves also with gauntlets, and of course, not to be overlooked, the pair of dark lens welding goggles. The goggles had two lenses. One was dark, one was clear. By lifting the dark lens upward, she was able to peer through the clear lens. The dark goggles, however, blocked the view of her dark brown eyes highlighted by purloined eye makeup. At the bottom was Hannah's bare feet with toenails painted a pastel pink.

Not to be overlooked were the ever-important canteens. No trip back in time would be possible without something to drink. They needed to be filled with water in case the intrepid explorers would be gone a long time, and they might get thirsty. That would also preclude a dose of Montezuma's revenge. Of course, they needed to pack something to eat. Hannah decided on a peanut butter and bread sandwich, no jelly. Sarah thought some ham would be nice, so she placed a packet of ham in their survival kit.

As they arranged themselves in the chair, barely able to avoid their recent additions to the piece of furniture, Sarah began explaining how everything worked. "Okay, Hannah. First we type in the date we want to visit. Then, to steer, we need to use the wheel on the record player. Using this arm as a lever will make us go faster or slower."

As she said that, she spun the turntable on the record player and moved the arm forward and back. "Then when we are ready to go, all we have to do is push this long key to start. Do you understand? Just don't push the bar unless we are both in the chair and ready to go. Okay?"

Honk. Honk. Honk. "That means yes," responded Hannah.

"Okay, Hannah. Are we ready to go?"

Honk. Honk. "That means no. I need to go get something I forgot." Having said that, she jumped out of the chair and headed for the junk pile. Digging around, Hannah picked up Grumpy's old cell phone and put it in her pocket. "I need my cell phone." As an afterthought, she also grabbed the clipboard and pencil.

Making herself comfortable in the chair, she took the clipboard and said, "Helmets?" She then picked up the pencil, made a check mark, and said, "Check."

"Goggles? Check." She made another mark on the clipboard.

"Headphones? Check."

"Gloves? Check."

"Scarf? Check."

"Horn? Check." *Honk. Honk. Honk.* Once again, Hannah penciled in another mark on the clipboard.

Completing her checklist, she reached up and squeezed the horn. *Honk. Honk. Honk.* "That means yes."

Having gotten the go-ahead from her copilot, Sarah tapped the date 1492 into the computer keyboard. She told Hannah, "Let's go see Columbus as he discovers America. We studied about him in school. I know all about

Columbus. This will be interesting. Is that okay?" Just as she was about to press the space bar on the computer that would send them back in time, she said, "Wait a minute. We forgot something very important!" With those words, she jumped out of the chair and headed for her bedroom.

While she was gone, Hannah was busy. "I never get to do what I want. Sarah always gets to do what she wants. She gets to cut the tape. I don't get to put anything on the chair. She gets to wear the helmet. She gets to pick where we are going. She gets to be the leader and drive. Why don't I get to do what I want?" Reaching over to the keyboard, she began to tap numbers on the computer. Just as she was about to hit the spacebar and send herself back in time without her sister, Sarah returned from the bedroom with two framed pictures. Climbing into the chair and arranging the photographs just so, she told Hannah, "We can't go on a new adventure without Grumpy and Grammy. They need to go with us. Grumpy would enjoy this adventure! He needs to be with us!"

With those words, Sarah reached for the computer and said to Hannah, "Are we ready now?"

Honk. Honk. Honk. "That means yes."

Sarah pulled her hand back and said, "Hannah, you push the button. You said you never get to do anything, so you get to push the button."

Hannah reached over with her gloved hand and began the countdown.

"Five…four…three…two…one." She pressed the space bar on the computer, and for good or bad, the adventure had begun.

CHAPTER FOUR

othing happened. No bang. No zoom. No swirling clouds. No rainstorm. Nothing. No thunder and lightning. Unquestionably, nothing happened. There they sat in the garage looking at the off-white walls and heavily laden shelves that surrounded them. "What happened? Hannah asked. "Why are we not going anywhere? What did you do wrong?"

Honk! Honk! "It wasn't my fault! I didn't do anything!" *Honk!*

Sarah was not distracted by her sister's commentaries or honking and began to go over everything they had done to ensure that nothing had been overlooked or that one of connections had come loose. After fiddling with the connections and checking the compass and turntable, she said, "Oh. Here is the problem! The chair is still in park! Look. All we have to do is move the arm on the record player forward and off we go. Ready?"

"See. I told you I didn't do anything." *Honk. Honk. Honk.* "That means yes."

With those three honks, Sarah moved the arm of the turntable forward. Again, no bang. No zoom. There was a small tremor in the chair that began to increase with each passing moment. The girls began to itch. There was a droning in their ears that grew louder and louder. Hannah exclaimed as she started to bail out of the chair, "I don't like this. I'm getting off. You can go by yourself!"

"No, Hannah, don't go. Stay. Just for a few more seconds. It will be all right. I promise! Stay."

Honk. Honk. "That means *no!*" No sooner were those honks out of her mouth than the chair began to move… But not like Sarah had thought it would. It started slowly at first and gathered speed with each passing second. What was surprising to Sarah was that the chair was going backward, and the speed was increasing. As the chair began its rearward movements, the lights in the garage began to flicker. The walls began to shimmy and wave like the quivering, faraway images on the asphalt of a hot highway. The floor began to undulate like the waves in a golden wheat field on a windy day. The humming grew so loud she thought the helmet on her head had become a beehive full of workers rushing around in a frenzy to prepare for a harsh winter.

With all this going on, Sarah felt Hannah wiggling and moving about in the chair. The chair was wobbling and fishtailing like a top that had run out of speed. She said, "Hannah, stop all that movement. Why are you so antsy? If you don't stop all that squirming around, you could cause us to miss our exit and there is no telling where we might end up. You could help me steer."

"Sarah, I have to potty. I really need to potty."

"We are going through a time vortex at the speed of light, and you have to potty? Why didn't you go before we left?

"Because I didn't have to before but I have to now!"

As the lights began to flicker brighter and brighter, the colors of the walls and the contents of the garage began to lose their color and became merely black and white. Moments later, the surroundings became black and white stripes. No sooner had the stripes appeared than the walls began to pucker in the middle and the rest of the walls began to swirl around faster and faster, like the storm circling around the eye of a hurricane gathering force. As the spinning grew, the stripes began to change into a spiraling black-and-white checkerboard that had lost its checkers.

Honk. Honk. Honk. Honk. Honk. "That means I want to go home!"

By now it was too late for either Sarah or Hannah to abandon ship. All they could do was to hang on the best way they were able and ride out the storm. Sarah was fighting for control by spinning the turntable this way and that way, but it seemed like it was a losing battle. It appeared she had lost control, and the best she could do was to keep the chair from crashing into a pillar of the time and space continuum. The storm continued to grow and grow. As the storm worsened, the time machine began to move in reverse faster and faster. Sarah thought that made sense. They were going back in time so the chair went backward.

The checkerboard continued to spin and began to take on an inky black appearance. The flickering lights began to go darker and finally became black. Sarah reached over and turned on the flashlight. Nothing! The meager light from the torch had absolutely no effect on the ebony pit of emptiness surrounding them. The beehive perched atop her head became more active, and the floor became so fluid the sisters were becoming seasick. Suddenly, everything stopped. No screeching of brakes. No sudden jerks. No skidding—just blackness and silence.

As Sarah sat in the chair trying to figure out what just happened and what course of action she should take, she heard from somewhere in the darkness that Hannah was moving around. Soon she heard her sister sigh, "Aah. That's more better." Sarah reached over for her little sister, but all she found was the empty spot in the chair. It was still warm so she had just recently gone missing.

Remaining in the chair, Sarah began to notice that the darkness around her was losing the inky, impenetrable stygian character and was beginning to lift just like a heavy fog bank. As the blackness lifted, a whole different landscape presented itself to her. Instead of being on a boat with Columbus crossing the endless blue ocean, she found herself alone on what appeared to be a small island in the middle of a river with tree-covered mountains surrounding her on all sides. It appeared to be early morning with a warm sun trying to remove the cool shadows that had been left by the previous night. Looking around, she could not see Hannah anywhere in sight. Did she jump off before they arrived at their destination? Was she left in some other place in time? Was she all by herself? How could Sarah explain to her mother that she had lost her sister somewhere between yesterday and the beginning of time? She was going to be in big trouble for a long time. She was glad she had a TV and some books in her bedroom.

Suddenly, she heard Hannah, "Sarah, I just pottied. I feel much better now."

Looking around with a relieved look on her face, she was unable to see her sister anywhere in sight. The relief changed to concern when she couldn't find her at all. She wondered whether she was only imagining that she heard Hannah's voice.

"I feel much better now. I didn't know if I was going to make it," continued Hannah.

"Where are you, Hannah? I don't see you."

"I'm down here in the water. Don't you see me? I just pottied in the river. I feel much better now!"

Looking around, Sarah still did not see her little sister. "Hannah, where are you?"

"Look down. I'm right here beside you." *Honk. Honk.*

All Sarah saw was a little muskrat in the shallows of the river. Taking a closer look, Sarah noticed that the muskrat was wearing a red hard hat with a bicycle horn taped to the top.

"Hannah, is that you?"

Honk. Honk. Honk. "That means yes."

"How did you get there? How did you become a muskrat?"

"I don't know, but this is great. Now I get to know what it's like to be…whatever I am."

"You're a muskrat. That's what you are. How are we going to explain this to Mom and Dad? How do we tell them they have a muskrat for a daughter?"

"Not us, Sarah. You! This was your idea. You get to tell them." *Honk. Honk.* "I guess I'll have to live in the bathtub."

"Hmmmm," mused Sarah. "This means I get to have the bedroom all to myself."

As the drama on the little island was unfolding, another performance was taking place. The predawn light breaking through the thinly veiled clouds had a promise of the day to come being very special. Frogs grumbled their farewell to the passing of another night, and the birds sang their ritual greetings to the new dawn as they have since the existence of time itself. Coming across to the little sandbar was a small boat with five men dressed in black. Pulling the boat up on the sand, they walked to the center of the island.

CHAPTER FIVE

T he new arrivals begrudgingly doffed their hats, and one of the men even walked over to Sarah. He was a very tall, very large man. He wasn't fat. Just big. His face was buried beneath a full, dark beard. Under his dark hat was a full head of long hair that reached to his shoulders. He gazed down at her and said, "Good morning. I'm Albert Pike. This is Mr. John Roane. We have some business to take care of. We will only be here for a short while. If you don't mind, young lady, stand over there out of the way so you won't be hurt. Thank you."

Having said his good morning to Sarah standing off to one side, he turned on his heels to rejoin the men at the center of the sandbar. They took no notice of the strange little muskrat in the hard hat by her feet. The men at the center of the sandbar took their places, two on each side and one in between them. Two of the men took off their coats and hats and handed them to the two gentlemen standing closest to them. Then the two men holding the coats took several steps back out of the way. The aristocratic-looking man who stood in the center, still with coat and hat, lifted a wooden box up to his chest, opened it, and waited. Then Sarah said to Hannah, "What do you suppose they are about to do?"

"I don't know, but it doesn't look very nice."

The two coatless men approached the man with the box and withdrew pistols from a wooden case. Sarah and her sister looked at one another with deep concern. They were still not sure what was about to happen, but it appeared not to be something of which their mother would approve.

The two men stood rigid, back-to-back. The man in the center set the wooden box on the ground and pulled a white linen handkerchief from his frock pocket and waited. The men wore somber, cold expressions on their faces. Both grasped a dueling pistol; their knuckles were white. As the steps were counted, each man took ten paces and stopped. Each man turned. Each man raised his arm, weapon extended. They each took aim. The man in the center dropped his handkerchief to the ground.

Boom boom.

The previously alive landscape became painfully quiet. The only sound then was the rippling of the water as it gently lapped around the sandbar. As the two clouds of black smoke cleared, the results of the shots become known. Both men missed!

Sarah had realized what was about to happen and told her sister to cover her ears. With the clearing of the smoke, she was still standing there with her hands over her ears and her mouth open in amazement. After taking in what had just transpired, she then looked around for Hannah. She was nowhere in sight! *Oh no. What could've happened?*

Where could she be? Instead of telling her parents that they had a muskrat for a daughter, she would have to tell them their rodent had been killed in a duel.

Suddenly she heard a splashing in the river and looked down at her feet. There was little sis crawling up on the sand. Her red helmet was sitting askew on her head, the horn was turned sideways and her goggles were hanging from her nose. Sitting there by Sarah's feet she said, "*Wow! I hope they don't do that again.*"

Foolish honor that had been the cause of many men's demise throughout history was still not satisfied. The pistols were refilled with black powder, followed by a round lead ball. Resuming their back-to-back stance, in the middle of the sandbar, with their arms raised, the count started once again. Both men took ten paces. Sarah shouted at Hannah, "They are going to do it again! Cover your ears!" Before those words were hardly out of her mouth, Hannah was again diving under the opaque water of the river.

As this was happening, both men turned. Again, they extended their weapons, aimed, and the man in the center again dropped his bandana.

Boom boom.

The sound of the gunfire returned from the sides of the mountains before the smoky haze had a chance to clear. In the thinning smoke, it became apparent to Sarah that once again both combatants had missed. At least they were both still standing. And once again the little muskrat returned to bank of the river. As Sarah looked down at Hannah, she couldn't help but smile. The red hard hat was now turned completely backward and the vortex goggles were dangling around her neck in front of her. "Are they done now?" she asked her big sister.

"I don't think so. They are loading the guns again."

"Oh no. Not again!"

By now, the sun had conspired with the night and had won the right to spread its warmth across the landscape. The men apparently had more difficulty sorting out their disagreement than the day and night had done just a few minutes earlier. So the pistols were once again reloaded. The ritual was repeated. Back-to-back. Nerves by now were frayed. Ten long paces. Fear began slithering up their spines. They turned. Arms tense, knuckles white. Aim. Vision blurry. *Pray!* The linen fabric was dropped. *Boom boom.* White clouds of smoke. Echoes of the gunfire surrounded the sandbar. Results? Sarah had her ears covered and was standing in a crouched position beside the riverbank, hoping this would soon be over. Hannah was missing again. Both men had missed for the third time.

About this time, the little muskrat slunk out of the water and hid behind Sarah's legs. Looking back, Sarah saw that the red hard hat was still backward and the bike horn was now hanging off to one side. The vortex goggles were at this point flopping around on Hannah's back as though the head strap was trying to strangle her. "Are they through yet?" asked Hannah.

"I sure hope they are because your vortex suit can't take much more of your diving in and out of the water. It's a good thing you know how to swim."

Honk. Honk. Honk, said the little horn. "That means yes," said Hannah.

Both of the men had missed again. That both men had displayed courage in the face of danger was apparently sufficient enough to settle the matter of a man's honor. The new day was dawning. The birds were singing their approval of the day. The sun was warming the landscape. Nerves were on edge. Maybe it was just a good day to be alive. Both men finally had the good sense to end their duel. As they shook hands, their seconds gathered up everything they had brought with them. The two men climbed back into their coats and patted their hats back on their heads. They looked over at Sarah and tipped their hats. They said their good-byes, climbed into the waiting boat, and rowed to the riverbank. There they disappeared as quietly as they had arrived only a few minutes earlier.

As Hannah began to put her vortex uniform back into some kind of order, she sighed and said, "I'm glad that's over! What was that all about?"

To this, Sarah could only shake her head and comment, "I don't have any idea. But I'm glad it's over too. Uhhh…Hannah. What did you do with the chair?"

"What chair?"

"The chair! You know, the time machine!"

"I haven't seen anything since the lights went out."

"Hannah, you must have done something to it. It's not here. Where is it?"

"How come I get blamed for everything? I was just sitting in the chair. It's too big for me to move. I didn't do anything with the chair. You must have lost it. Not me."

"Hannah, I didn't do anything with the chair, and you didn't do anything with the chair. So where is it? How will we get home?"

As the two sisters stood on the small sandbar in the middle of the wilderness, they were wondering what they could do when Hannah said, "I know!" With those two words, their troubles were solved. She reached into her pocket and removed Grumpy's old cell phone. She said, "All I have to do is call the phone that you put in the arm of the chair. It's that simple."

"Oh, Hannah. That's silly. You don't even know the number on the chair's phone. How can you call?"

"I do so know the number. Watch!" With those words, she opened the phone and began poking in numbers. She punched in numbers until she thought she had enough to call the other phone. Hitting the send button, she waited. Suddenly, as if by magic—make that imagination—the chair appeared beside them. "See. Nothing to it!" exclaimed Hannah with a smirk on her face.

The girls climbed aboard the ugly old chair. They arranged themselves in their preordained positions. Sarah punched the current date in the computer keyboard, and just before pushing the space bar, she said, "How will we explain to Mom that one of us is a muskrat?"

"Not us. You." *Honk. Honk. Honk.*

With the final strokes of the buttons, the chair began its journey back to the present time. This time, the chair moved forward and not back since they were going ahead in time. As blackness enveloped them, Sarah wondered what had happened. For some unknown reason, they had not met with Columbus like she had wanted. Something was not right, but she would worry about it later.

When they got home, Sarah was curious as to the adventure that they had witnessed and began to look on the Internet and in some history books that were at home. What had transpired was a sort of a "fancified" version of the famous "Sandbar Duel."

- General Albert Pike had served in the Mexican War with another rival officer, John S. Roane, a Van Buren attorney before the war and future fourth Governor of Arkansas. Apparently, Albert Pike and Mr. Roane publicly blamed each other for the conduct of Arkansas troops during the war. Finally, General Pike issued a challenge, and Mr. Roane accepted. The result was the famous "Sandbar Duel." The actual exchange of gunfire took place in 1848, on a sandbar in the Arkansas River somewhere between Fort Smith and the Indian Territory. In actuality both men fired and missed twice. While waiting for the pistols to be reloaded for the third time, the duelists' surgeons were able to arrange an agreement that settled the matter of honor. Of course, the fact that a round ball parted General Pike's beard and a ball had zipped through Mr. Roane's ear may have had something to do with the settlement. After the smoke cleared, calmer heads prevailed and they shook hands, had breakfast together, and became friendly for the rest of their lives.

- Duels at this time were illegal, and it was the last recorded duel held in Arkansas. Duels were common throughout history. From knights banging away on each other with swords or other disgusting implements of war to settling matters of honor with pistols, duels have been around for a long time. Kings in Europe banned duels because they were losing too many of their royalty and would either banish or execute anyone found on the dueling field. At one point, the king of France lost over four thousand of his best military and noble men to duels in a ten-year period. Because of the the inaccuracy of dueling pistols, there were more lives lost in duels by sword, épées, and rapiers than were lost with the use of firearms.

- In America, dueling became a popular pastime. From the founding of the United States of America to the Civil War, the US Navy lost more officers to duels than were lost in enemy action. By some accounts, Andrew Jackson was involved in as many as one hundred duels in his lifetime.

- Duels were a matter of honor and followed a certain prescribed protocol. This protocol varied from country to country, from different parts of the same country, or the type of weapon agreed to by the combatants. The weapon could be sword, pistol, knife, fist, or any weapon chosen by the "wronged" party. The offended individual had his pick of weapons. Usually there was a referee whose responsibility it was to oversee the actual duel and ensure that it was conducted properly and according to the guidelines established by the "seconds."

- Seconds were the ones who did the actual arrangements of the duel. They selected the time, place, weapons, referee, etc. The combatants communicated with each other through their seconds. It would not be proper or even wise to have the two combatants working out the particulars to settle the matter of honor themselves. The seconds would also try to find a less violent means to settle any differences, if possible. Usually, there was not alternative method that both parties could agree upon. Seconds would also hold the hats and coats of the heroes during the actual duel. It was also not unheard of for the seconds to suddenly become involved in the duel itself.

Eventually, the effects of time travel had worn off Hannah. She was once again her normal self. The girls did not have to explain to their parents why they had a muskrat for a daughter. She did not have to live in the bathtub, and Sarah did not get the bedroom all to herself. Sarah still had not been able to find anything wrong with the chair and could not find any reason they had ended up in the wrong time.

CHAPTER SIX

Hannah was up early for a Saturday. She was attired in her PJs, an old faded robe from Grumpy's childhood, and a pair of fuzzy slippers. Her hair was still tangled and full of bird nests from an energetic sleep. Sarah was still asleep. It had been a long evening at the school skate party the night before. While waiting for her big sister to get up, Hannah turned on the TV and was trying to find one of Scooby Doo's adventures. Unable to find any Scooby mysteries, she settled on a cartoon that she hadn't seen before. Maybe she would have Sarah show her how to start the VCR when she got out of bed.

Before much longer, Sarah came groggily down the hallway barefoot and clad in her Selena Gomez T-shirt from the night before. As she plunked down on the sofa, Hannah held out the remote and asked, "Sarah, please find Scooby Doo for me." Sarah took the offered remote from her and shuffled through the channels, but there was still no Scooby exploit on any of the stations. Hannah said in an earnest tone, "I want to watch Scooby Doo!"

"Hannah, Scooby is not on. We will have to watch something else! What else do you want?"

"Scooby Doo! I want to watch Scooby!"

"Hannah, it's not on. We can't watch what's not on. There is nothing we can do. We will have to do something else. I've got a great idea! Let's get in the time machine and go someplace interesting! Okay?"

"Sarah, I'm thirsty. Please get me something to drink."

Sarah slowly got off the couch and shambled her way into the kitchen to get Hannah a glass of orange juice. Handing the glass of juice to her sister, she said, "Would you like to go back in time?"

"Sure, after I finish drinking my juice."

"Great! You finish the juice, and I'll make some snacks to take with us. What do you want to eat?"

"Actually, I just want some peanut butter and bread, no jelly. Okay?"

Sarah went into the kitchen and fixed a peanut butter and bread sandwich for Hannah. Since there was no packet of ham in the fridge she decided the next best thing would be a bag of chips. With the lunch menu decided, it was time to get suited up in their time vortex attire. Hannah had finished her juice and put on her uniform for the trip much like last time. There she stood in red hard hat with horn that had been reattached, welder's goggles, scarf, and gloves. To complete this garb, she was still wearing her old robe that was faded beyond color recognition and her furry slippers. She was ready to meet the challenges of the day. Next to her was Sarah. Starting off in her blue Selena Gomez T-shirt and bare feet, she added her tanker helmet, goggles, yellow scarf, and large gloves. The two sisters were quite a flamboyant pair of time explorers.

The courageous voyagers headed out to the garage where they stowed their lunches, climbed aboard their time craft, and settled in for exploration through the fabric of time itself. Once ensconced in their proper places, Sarah said, "Let's go back to the ride of Paul Revere. We studied all about him in school." Having decided that, she entered the date 1775 in the computer keyboard. "Are we ready, Hannah?"

Hannah picked up her clipboard and began her checklist. "Helmets? Check."

"Horn? Check."

"Earphones? Check."

"Goggles? Check."

"Grumpy's cell phone? Check."

"Scarf? Check."

"Gloves? Check." After each comment, she made a check mark on the clipboard. Then laying the pencil and board down, she said, "Checklist is done."

Sarah said, "Okay, are we ready to go?'

Honk. Honk. Honk. "That means yes."

"Oh wait, Hannah. I need to get something I forgot!" She jumped up and headed for her bedroom.

While she was away, Hannah began to grouse. "She always gets to pick where we get to go. I never get to pick. I don't get to do anything I want to do. It's not fair. I have good ideas too," said Hannah as she reached over to the keyboard and began typing in numbers at random. She pulled her hand back just before Sarah returned to the garage wearing her flip-flops. A time traveler cannot travel in time barefooted.

Assuming her position beside Hannah in the big, old chair, Sarah asked, "Are we ready?"

Honk. Honk. Honk.

"Okay, here we go." Sarah hit the spacebar on the computer, moved the arm on the record player out of park, and once again they were off into the maelstrom of time tourism. As it happened before, the chair began to tremble and vibrate. The girls began to itch like dozens of spiders were crawling all over their skin. The droning in their heads began to increase and the chair began to gather speed as it began to move backward. The walls turned black and white and began their wild and crazy dance of spiraling into a checkerboard. The lights began to flicker faster and faster as the chair continued to increase its speed from inches to feet to yards per seconds. Soon the floor began to rumble and shimmy, and the humming increased in volume.

Everything went black. It was like being swallowed by a black-and-white plaid whale.

"Sarah, I'm hungry. Can we eat now?"

"Hannah, look where we are! We are about to enter the time warp and now you have to eat. Why didn't you eat before we left? We can't eat now. It's hard enough steering without you trying to find your sandwich. You will just have to wait."

"My tummy hurts. I don't feel good. I need something to eat. I want to go home."

Suddenly the storm abated. All was quiet. Nothing moved. The oppressive blackness hung over the time travelers like being at the bottom of a deep well at night during a storm. The air was heavily laden with moisture that seemed to wrap around their bodies like a heavy wet, soggy dish rag. They heard water moving and sloshing. Maybe they really were at the bottom of a well.

CHAPTER SEVEN

As the darkness began to fade, Sarah did not see Hannah. Not only could she not find her sister, but it was becoming apparent that this was not the place where she would find Paul Revere. She again wondered what went wrong. Scanning the area in search for her little sister, she was able to see a lot of men grouped together. They were dressed rather strangely. What once must have been colorful and bright clothing was now rags. Many of them wore various items of armor such as helmets and breastplates that were rusty and in disrepair.

Sarah whispered, "Hannah, where are you? Can you hear me? Where did you go?" Her only reply was the chirping of the local birds that were coming alive with the awaking of a new day. Soon the other animals began to stir, and life returned to the landscape as it had for as long as history itself.

Finally, the sun cracked the imprisoning darkness, and the order was given to shoulder their tools, gather up their cargo, and start the climb up the side of the hill. The man who looked most important handed Sarah a shovel and waited. His dented and scarred armor had a reddish tint due to unattended care. His dark beard and mustache was streaked with white and was no longer trimmed but rather shaggy and matted. Surrounding his neck was a very tall collar with the remnants of lace that had seen better days. His dark eyes appeared tired and worn from carrying the responsibility of command.

Sarah was unsure of what to do next. She was still worried about her little sister. The bearded man in rusty armor stood there looking at her until she fell in line with the members of the assembled men. The cargo was, until just a short time ago, one of their shipmates.

As they began to cross an open area in complete silence, Sarah heard an obnoxious but welcome sound. *Honk. Honk. Honk. Honk.* "That means hi." Sarah looked around but did not see the source of the honking. "Sarah, here I am. Don't you see me? I'm in the tree!" Hannah giggled.

As she looked up into the trees, Sarah spotted a robin wearing, of all things, a red hard hat with horn attached. "What are you doing up there?"

"Well, I was hungry, so I was over there eating some berries. I'm full now. They were good!"

Sarah impatiently explained, "Hannah, robins do not eat berries. They eat worms!"

"Oh. I'm just a little kid. How am I supposed to know? Besides, I don't like worms! But I do like berries." *Honk. Honk. Honk.*

About that time the bearded man came upon Sarah and told her to be quiet. He told her they did not want problems with the savage people who lived nearby. She was to keep quiet and keep moving. As he turned and started across the open space in the forest, there sounded an irritating noise.

Honk. Honk. Honk. "That means okay."

The bearded man spun around and glared at Sarah. She could only give a sheepish grin and shrugged her shoulders. He pointed his finger at Sarah, brought his finger to his lips, turned, and crossed the open expanse. He disappeared from her sight as he entered the tree line on the other side.

Sarah looked up at the robin in the tree and whispered angrily, "You always get me into trouble. You do something and I get blamed for it. You make up stories and everybody blames me. It's not fair."

The bird replied, "I didn't do anything. I'm just a robin sitting in a tree." *Honk. Honk.*

"Hannah, be quiet. That mean man will come back, and I'll be in more trouble because of you."

Honk. Honk. Honk.

"Hannah!"

As the journey continued, the carefully chosen footsteps of the pallbearers still crunched on the stones and the underbrush. The noise was loud enough to rouse the just-awakened birds to take flight and the frogs and other slithery life to scamper for the safety of the riverbank.

The distance was not all that far. It was only a short climb up the steep side of the hill laced with lush vegetation and trees of all flavors. Occasionally, small animals startled the already edgy men. Sarah was having no trouble keeping up. She just remembered what her Grumpy had said a long time ago when they explored some cliffs: "If I can do it, you can do it." These words helped her up the mountain side.

Hannah was enjoying the morning. She flitted from one tree to the next, honking her horn from wherever she perched. At every honk, Sarah would cringe and expect the bearded man to return and admonish her for the racket her sister was making. Frequently, she would try to silence Hannah, but her scolding had absolutely no effect. After about thirty or forty minutes they arrived at their destination.

The burial site had been selected the previous day. It was most of the way up the hillside on a small flat area surrounded by trees. The prevailing winds carried the damp air from the river up the hillside, swaying the tall grass and trees. It overlooked the river as it made its way to the mighty Mississippi. Rocky ground would make digging difficult. Sarah helped the men dig as deep as they were able and then they laid the body to rest. They realized that animals would dig up the remains easily, so they placed large stones at the head and feet. More large stones anchored the sides and capped off the top of the grave, forming a small crypt. A priest clad in a dirty and ragged brown robe that seemed to Sarah to be too large for his lanky build. The once neatly tonsured head had an un-kept look as did his now sunken face beneath his dark, calm eyes. Above his eyes were the bushiest eyebrows Sarah had ever seen. In his small, soiled hands he held a well-worn rosary. He bowed his head and said a prayer for their fallen companion. After he finished, he turned to the bearded man, who had chided Sarah to be quiet, and said, "Señor De Soto, would you like to say a few words before we leave?"

De Soto nodded his head, stepped toward the crypt with a determined stride, and talked about how brave the man had been. He talked about the man's loyalty and said that he would be missed. After he said his soft words, he turned to the men beside the grave and barked, "Let us go back, get the others, and move out of the cursed place."

The tools were gathered up and the trip back to their camp was made in silence, except for the occasional honks from the robin that kept pace with the detail of men. Arriving at camp, they collected their equipment and the men they had left to guard it; they continued on with their exploration.

Sarah placed herself at the end of the army and began to lag until the men were out of sight and sound. As she looked around and listened, she noticed the insufferable robin that was making life unbearable by all the tooting. Hannah said, "Well, they are gone. Now what do we do?"

Sarah answered, "We find the chair and get out of here. That's what we do! Where is the chair?"

"I don't know, Sarah, but I can call it on the phone." She pulled the phone from somewhere on her person and began to punch in numbers at random. With a flip of the wrist, she closed the phone and said, "Done."

No sooner were the words out of her mouth than the chair appeared in a choking swirl of dust. When the dust cleared, the duo climbed into the chair and prepared for their trip back home. As Sarah entered the current time into the computer, she said to Hannah, "I wonder what is wrong. I set the time for Paul Revere, and we went to the wrong time again. What could be causing that?"

"I don't know, Sarah. I didn't do anything," said Hannah innocently. *Honk. Honk.*

So with a push of the button, the sisters returned forward in time and arrived safely home just in time for the lunch that their mother had fixed. As they were eating, Sarah asked her mother, "Who was De Soto?"

Her mother replied, "De Soto was a Spanish explorer. They were called Conquistadors. He was the first known European to discover the Mississippi River. The story has it that De Soto and his men came through this area. You may remember Grumpy talking about De Soto passing very near to where we live."

Sarah said, "Oh, now I remember. We had that adventure to the cemetery down the hill from Grumpy's house, and we searched and found the 'Panther Head Rock.' I remember."

"Why do you ask about De Soto?"

"Oh, no reason. I was just wondering."

Mom said, "If you are really interested, why don't you look him up in the encyclopedia? If you look up De Soto for yourself, you will remember more about him."

"I think I will as soon as I'm through eating lunch. Thanks, Mom."

After finishing her lunch, Sarah went into the living room and pulled the D volume of the encyclopedia from the book shelf and took it out to the garage. She climbed into the big old chair and opened the tome to De Soto. She sat there with a slight smile on her lips and remembered. Sitting in the chair brought back memories of the many adventures that she and her Grumpy had not so long ago. It was almost like he was sitting right next to her once again.

With misty eyes, she started reading about De Soto.

- Hernando De Soto (1500–1542) was born in Spain, and at the age of thirty-two, he joined the conquistador Francisco Pizarro on the exploration and conquest of Peru. After enduring many months of hard fighting, the Spanish retired from Peru with Indian slaves and riches in gold.

- He settled down to life as a wealthy man but found daily life dull and boring. The Holy Roman Emperor (who was also King Charles I of Spain) named him Governor of Cuba, and in 1538, he sailed for the new world with supplies and about seven hundred men and two hundred horses. Landing in Cuba, they immediately set out on further exploration of the New World. They crossed over to Florida and landed about where Tampa Bay is located today.

- They marched inland and happened upon an Indian who was in fact a Spaniard named Juan Ortiz who was captured by the Indians some twelve years earlier. He became their guide and interpreter. De Soto led his men on a wide sweep, looking for gold and other treasures, through what would become Georgia, North and South Carolina, Mississippi, and Tennessee. Crossing the Mississippi River about where Memphis is now located, they continued on through Arkansas and Oklahoma before retreating back to the coast.

- De Soto died on the return trip near the Mississippi River in 1542, and his men secretly buried him deep in the Mississippi River so that the Indians would not find his body. The surviving members of the expedition then numbered only about three hundred. After many hardships, the remnants of the army were able to arrive at a Spanish town in present-day Mexico. They had found not a bit of treasure, and most of the time, they had trouble locating enough food to eat. Sarah sat there and remembered the story Grumpy had told her not too long ago.

- Did what Sarah and Hannah saw actually take place? According to her Grumpy, the local legend said it did. The details of her adventure may not quite be historical, but according to the local myths, the crypt in Fairview Cemetery on the east side of Highway 59 (Log Town Hill to the Van Buren, Arkansas, residents) belongs to one of De Soto's conquistadors. One of many who died on the march through the strange new world. De Soto lost almost seventy percent of the men he began the expedition with, including his own life. On an oddly constructed grave are strange markings on the headstone that have almost faded from view. On the foot stone is a brass plate that tells the interested reader that here lies a soldier of De Soto. The stone sides to the grave are still intact, but the stones that covered the grave have long gone. If the story is true, then Fairview Cemetery in Van Buren, Arkansas, might be the oldest Christian grave west of the Mississippi River.

- The panther head rock that Sarah had mentioned can be found in Greenwood, Arkansas, in Bell Park. Back in the1930s, a man claimed to have a map drawn by the Indians. It seems that the Indians heard of De Soto's army approaching and had heard that he was very interested in gold and other valuables. To protect their valuables, they buried everything on the edge of a mountain under a rock that looked like a panther's head. He spent a good part of his life blasting and digging for the treasure. All of his time and effort were wasted. He never did find his pot of gold. The once-large hole has been filled in by time and is now only a dimple on the landscape. The panther head is still watching over the lost Indian treasurer. It has been weathered over the years, but the head jutting out from the large rock is still visible today on the bluff of the mountain overlooking the town of Greenwood.

Grumpy liked the myths so well that he never had any intention of proving or disproving them. Another theory about the grave is that the faded and worn writing on the stone was in effect runes for earlier Norse explorers. Grumpy always thought the Desoto explanation was the preferred theory. Sarah thought with a grin on her face and a tear in her eye that she could live with the stories as well.

CHAPTER EIGHT

I t was finally another Saturday morning. To Sarah, it was a free day. No school. No church. This was her day to do just as she pleased. While waiting for Hannah to recover from staying up all night and half the morning, she perused through the encyclopedias trying to find just the right place in time to visit as soon as Hannah decided to join the living. As she leafed through the different volumes of the many books, one jumped out and grabbed her attention. *Titanic!* That would be a wonderful adventure. It was the largest, fastest, and most elegant ship of the White Star Lines and was considered unsinkable. But it sank. They could find out exactly how the unsinkable sank. The day was decided. She knew what they were going to do today.

Going into the kitchen, she fixed them some snacks that would sustain the travelers on their current quest. As always, a peanut butter and bread sandwich, no jelly, and a banana for Hannah. As she sifted through the refrigerator for an easy snack, she found a small Tupperware container with macaroni and cheese. Her favorite! She loaded them into a sack and stowed the sack in the chair. Now all she had to do was wait for Hannah to awaken, and their quest would begin.

While she waited, she thought it might be nice to get the vortex uniforms out of the closet. Entering their shared bedroom, she opened the closet door and began to gather up the required items. Of course, if she accidently made enough noise doing that, Hannah just might wake up. Sarah began singing and banging doors, drawers, and dropping heavy things onto the floor.

It took some doing, but the sleeping partner in time travel began to wake up. Looking over, she saw Sarah singing and glancing occasionally over to the bed. Hannah pulled the covers over her head and said, "Sarah, go away! I need more sleep!"

Sarah, however, was not to be put off. She began to make even more racket and to sing even louder. As Hannah pulled the pillow over her head, Sarah said, "Wake up! I have a good adventure waiting for us. Let's go. Wake up!"

Hannah continued to moan and flop around on the bed. "Let me sleep. I'm tired. Go away!" groused Hannah.

"Hannah, I have a snack packed and our time suits all laid out. Get up! I'll make you breakfast of egg yolk and toast!"

How could she resist her favorite food in the world? Hannah threw the covers off and her feet hit the floor running. As she left the room, she said, "I'm hungry. I want yolk and toast."

Fixing Hannah her breakfast, Sarah decided to make some scrambled eggs for herself. As the sisters ate their eggs, Sarah told little sis about the adventure that was planned for the day. Sarah explained the sinking of the ocean liner after colliding with an iceberg in the Atlantic Ocean. They would pay a visit to the *Titanic* and observe the events of that fateful day.

After putting away their dishes, they went to their bedroom to get dressed for the voyage into another time. The attire was much like it had been for the other exploits of time travel. Helmet or hard hat with horn attached, goggles, earphones, cell phone, and heavy leather gloves. To her uniform, Sarah added a compass that Grumpy had given her. This she hung around her neck by the handy lanyard that was attached to the compass. Not to be out done, Hannah added a flashlight to her wardrobe. She said, "The *Titanic* sank at night. I need this to see at night when it gets dark." She then taped the flashlight to the right side of her hard hat, right next to the horn. By now the hard hat was now almost as much tape as hat. She placed the hat on her head, and the weight of the flashlight caused the hat to shift down to the right side of her head. Every time she pushed the hat back in place, it would immediately slide back down until its movement was arrested by her ear. In any case, she was now ready for just about any difficulty that might arise. That's what mattered.

As they sauntered out to the garage, Sarah said, "Remember the old movie we saw last night about the spaceship they called the *Enterprise*? I think we ought to call the chair 'the Grumpy.' What do you think?"

Honk. Honk. Honk. "That means yes," said Hannah as she pushed the hat/horn/flashlight off her ear. The hat immediately slid back down and rested on her ear once again.

The time trekkers entered the garage, boarded the Grumpy, and Sarah entered the date 1912 into the computer. She asked, "Hannah, are you ready to go?"

The answer was *honk, honk, honk.*

Sarah pushed the spacebar on the computer. Nothing happened. No humming. No spinning walls. No nothing. The just sat there in the middle of the garage.

Hannah said, "I didn't do nothing. It's not my fault." *Honk. Honk. Honk. Honk.*

Sarah moved the turntable arm forward and backward. Still nothing. She spun the turntable. Nothing. She retyped the date and hit the spacebar again. But in her haste, she typed in 1822 and not 1912. Still nothing happened. Nada. "What did you do, Hannah? It worked okay the last time we used it."

"I didn't do nothing."

"You must have because it's not working!" said Sarah as she began to check all the connections. Finding nothing wrong, she sat there for a minute thinking. She had no idea what was wrong.

Hannah said, "Maybe the clock. Sarah, check the clock."

"Hannah! That's a dumb idea. The clock is right here where it's always been." Reaching into the arm of the chair, she picked up the alarm clock and showed it to Hannah.

"Is it ticking?" asked Hannah.

Sarah placed the clock next to her ear and listened for the ticking. "Oh. No, it's not," said Sarah as she began to wind the clock.

Honk. Honk. Honk. Honk. Honk. Honk. "That means 'I didn't do nothing, but I fixed it," gloated Hannah. *Honk. Honk. Honk.*

With the time problem fixed, Sarah again hit the button on the computer, moved the arm of the record player, and they were off on the next adventure. Once again the humming commenced, the walls began to spin, and the black-and-white plaid whale once again swallowed the travelers, chair and all. Sarah heard, "Oh no! Sarah, I need to…" Then complete darkness and silence.

CHAPTER NINE

"**H**annah! Hannah! Are you okay? Where are you? Hannah! What did you need?"

"Sarah, I need to fasten my seat belt. I didn't fasten my belt before we left."

"We don't have seat belts. We never put them on the chair. That's a good idea. When we get back home we can put them on the chair. Just hang on tight for now."

Hannah said, "Okay, I'll hang on the best I can. You should have put seat belts on when we made this thing. It is all your fault, Sarah!"

After a couple of hard bumps, everything was still and very quiet. Before long, the darkness began to lift like the curtain on an opening act at a stage play. Along with the fading of the darkness came the chorus of excited voices, all talking at once. With the coming of daylight, Sarah was able to take in her surroundings.

She was standing in a wide dirt street lined with horses and carriages. At the far end of the road was a large crowd of people. Walking to the street she joined the throng of milling people. Some of the people were attired in clean pressed suits and dresses. Others appeared to have left their plows in the corn fields or to have just dried their hands from the wash tub. Children were running through the mingling people and barking dogs at their heels rounded out the crowd. The people were extremely excited about something. They bumped and elbowed each other, trying to gain just the right location. Gathered at the end of a town at the edge of a steadily moving river, everyone one was talking in loud and animated voices. Sarah noticed that the surrounding mountains and the water's edge looked vaguely familiar. She was not sure where, but she knew that she should have known the location. Further looking about, she noticed that people were everywhere. There were spectators on the roofs of buildings. Some were in the forks and branches of the nearby trees. Some were gathered in and around boats tied up to the riverbank. Children were weaving in and out through the constantly changing seas of adults. People were everywhere! Except for one very important person. Hannah was nowhere in sight!

She moved about the excited, constantly mingling sea of humanity that surrounded her. As she made her way through the crowd, she called out Hannah's name. Making the circuit of the gathered throng a couple of times, she still did not find Hannah or any indication that she was anywhere near. She did not find her sister, but she heard a lot of comments from the crowd. "This is a most wondrous age that we live in!" "There are advances made every day." "What will come next?" "Life will improve around here now." "Isn't progress wonderful?" These and many more comments were heard by Sarah as she tried to desperately to locate her little sister.

Suddenly everyone peered out along the river. All eyes were squinted against the dazzling sun as it reflected off the ruffling water as it continued its ever constant passage to foreign places hidden around every twist and turn. Every neck was craned, and eyes were straining up the river. The mass of people was eager with anticipation as well as fascination. Word had reached them that this great event was heading in their direction. No one wanted to miss this historic occasion. Suddenly, from the top of one of the buildings someone shouted, "Out there, just around the bend in the river!"

All eyes scanned the flank of the river just where it made the long, slow curve to the right. There it was. The belching black telltale smoke could be seen above the tree-lined water. Even before the vessel hoved into view, the screeching of a steam whistle announced its arrival. The dying echoes of the whistle blast mingled with the cheers, whoops, and discharged firearms of the expectant crowd as the white prow of the steamer magically rounded the bend. The steamer headed directly to the constantly growing crowd that congregated at the banks of the river.

Momentarily caught up with the excitement of the horde, Sarah forgot about her lost sister. She became just one of the many eager onlookers in a packed gathering. Staring out over the water, she watched as the ship approached the gathered masses. As the steamship neared the crowd, the thudding of the engine suddenly decreased and the sloshing, chopping paddle wheel noticeably slowed down. The paddle wheel no longer chopped at the water's surface with a vengeance but continued with an almost gentle flutter of waves.

As the boat eased its struggle with the current, it slowly began to edge to the bank of the river. The foaming wake lapped at the water's edge. The steam whistle again shrieked its welcome and large ropes were tossed to men standing along the bank. With a shuttering of the mechanical demons within the bowels of the ship and the final wash of the rippling water, the steamboat was at rest. On the side of the boat was the name *Robert Thompson* in bold letters. Behind the Robert Thompson were two smaller boats lashed to the larger boat like the freight cars to a locomotive. All were loaded to the hilt with boxes, barrels, crates, and assorted containers. It was apparent to Sarah that the arrival heralded a new era for the residents of town.

With the commencement of the speeches of the local dignitaries and the start of the celebration, Sarah once again began to investigate the loss of her little sister. *Why can't Hannah stay with me? It would make everything much easier. Hey…wait a minute. That's not the Titanic! What happened? Something very strange is going on.*

Deciding to retrace her footsteps, she began the arduous trek through the mass of milling spectators. Before she could reach the location at which she started, she heard a *honk, honk, honk, honk.* Not sure if she heard correctly, she stopped and listened very intently. From a short distance away was a *honk, honk, honk.* Sure enough, there it was again!

Following the honking like Hansel and Gretel following bread crumbs, she found herself standing next to the newly arrived boat. Searching the area, Sarah was still unable to locate Hannah. Sarah was beginning to get a very bad feeling about this whole adventure. First, this was not the *Titanic*. Second, Hannah was missing again. Third, the chair was missing again. Fourth, the—*Honk. Honk.*

As Sarah looked around, she was still unable to find any trace of Hannah. *Honk. Honk.* "Up here, Sarah." Hannah giggled.

As Sarah looked up, she saw the source of the honks sitting on the deck of the boat. Inspecting a little more closely, Sarah noticed a red hard hat. On that hard hat was a bicycle horn and flashlight attached with duct tape. Beneath the cocked hat was a tabby cat grinning at her with all available teeth. "Hannah, is that you? Why didn't you answer me when I called? Where have you been? Where is the chair? I was worried about you! Don't do that to me again! Well... say something. Don't just sit there staring at me!" Sarah finally quit talking when she noticed that she was getting strange looks from the individuals standing close to her and Hannah.

Taking Hannah in tow, Sarah led her to the far end of the boat. When they got to the end, Sarah said, "Well, say something. I know it's you, Hannah. Why did you not answer me?"

"You're not the boss of me!" said Hannah. *Honk. Honk. Honk.*

"Yes, I am, Hannah. At least until we get home! Now tell me!"

"Okay. Actually, I just arrived on the boat. I got bumped out of the chair on the last big bump. I landed on top of the boat, and suddenly, I was drinking milk from a bowl. I did not get very much milk because that loud screeching scared me, and I ran off and hid under a bed. After it got quiet, I sneaked out here and here I am. Aren't you proud of me?"

"I was afraid I lost you. Why can you not stay with me?"

"It wasn't my fault. The chair bumped me out! It was your fault because you didn't put seat belts in the chair. Don't blame me!" *Honk. Honk.*

"Hannah! Stop honking at me! We will put seat belts in the chair when we get back home. Right now we need—Did you say you were drinking milk? You know you can't drink milk. All I need is a lactose intolerant cat to take care of."

"I didn't drink much. That shrieking scared me, and I hid under the bed," said Hannah.

"Well, I'm not changing your cat litter! What will Mom and Dad say? What will our dog, Molly, think? Oh, Hannah. You cause me more trouble!"

"I didn't do nothing!"

"Hannah! Right now, we need to find out where we are and what's happening. This place looks familiar, but I'm not sure from where," said Sarah as a man and woman strolled past, inspecting the newly arrived vessel. The muscular man was young, of average height, and was wearing a dark coat and vest. His white shirt sported pearl buttons that matched the stick pin in his lapel. Set in the middle of his rawboned face was a black handlebar mustache. He tipped his wide brimmed hat at Sarah. The young lady was attired in a pretty green gown that swept the ground as she passed by. A matching bonnet covered her long brown hair that was put up in a bun. Completing her ensemble was a white parasol to keep the sun away from her fair skin. As the couple walked by, they paused and stared at Sarah as if her brains were slowly oozing out of her ears. She asked Sarah, "Are you talking to me, young lady?"

Sarah could only grin and look about. She said, "No, ma'am. I'm talking to my little sister. You know they can be a bother sometimes."

The woman continued to stare at Sarah in disbelief. "I don't see any sister. Do you feel all right?"

Sarah could only stammer, "Did I say my sister? I meant to say my cat. See, here is my cat."

As Sarah and the couple looked around, there was not a sister or a cat in sight. Sarah was standing there alone. Hannah had disappeared again. The woman said to Sarah, "Hmmm…I think you have been out in the sun without your bonnet. You need to have a drink of water and go over and sit in the shade." The couple then turned and continued with their inspection of the boat with occasional backward glances at Sarah and some hushed tones about the strange little girl standing all by herself at the water's edge.

By now Sarah was red-faced and frantically looking around for her little sister. Suddenly she saw the tail of a cat disappear into a doorway about halfway down the length of the ship. Sarah tried to scale the side of the boat. It was too tall, and there was no place for her to place her feet for a boost. Off went Sarah in pursuit of the disappearing tail.

Racing down the length of the ship, she came to a sliding halt by the gangway that stretched from the boat deck to the nearest point on shore. Pausing to look both ways, she cautiously began to slink across the wooden access. Arriving onboard, she stood there trying to remember what door her cat had entered when a tall gentleman appeared and blocked her entry. His medium frame was softened by age but still retained a trim muscular appearance. His simple uniform was a dark blue with a white shirt and a black string tie that hung around his stiff collar. On his broad shoulders were gold epaulettes with matching gold braid encircling his jacket cuffs. Finishing out his dapper uniform were two rows of matching gold buttons down the front of his coat. He was certainly someone of importance. As she looked up into the stern, dark, weather-worn face, she knew she was in deep trouble. All thanks to her little sister.

CHAPTER TEN

"Er…ah…ah…er…ohhh," stammered Sarah.

"Hello, young lady. What brings you to my ship?" said the stern face.

"Well…er…ah…well."

"Come, come. You must be here for a reason. Do you plan on robbing the ship?"

"Oh, *no*, sir!" said Sarah.

"Are you running away from home? Are you trying to seek a ride on my boat? Speak up! What do you want?"

"Oh, no, sir!" said Sarah. "I've lost my sister, and I think she is on your boat."

"Well, young lady, I can assure you no one has come aboard. I've been standing here ever since we docked and nobody has come on board."

"Did I say sister? I meant to say I lost my cat. That's what I meant. My cat is lost. I don't have a sister. Have you seen my cat?" asked Sarah.

"Which is it? Cat or sister? There is a big difference of what we need to be on the lookout for."

"My cat. I've lost my cat."

"Well, let me see. The only cat I've seen on board is the one that lives here. Her name is Hannah. She is a good mouser. We keep her on board to catch any mice or rats. Does a real good job of it. In fact, I just saw her chase a mouse into that cabin right down there," said the tall man.

"What does she do after she catches them?"

"Why, I suppose she eats them. All we give her is some milk when we have it. Other than that, she pretty much takes care of herself."

"Oh dear! I have to rescue her. Where did you say she went, mister?" asked Sarah with concern in her voice. She just had to save her sister from eating a rat. *Ugh*!

"Save who from what? I'm the captain of this boat. My name is Philip Pennywit. If anybody does any saving here, it will be me."

"I have to get to Hannah before she has a chance to eat the rat. If I let her eat that rat, my parents will be very unhappy. She will get sick. I'll be in big trouble. Besides, she has already had a bowl of milk and she can't drink milk. The litter box will be full. Please help me!"

The captain asked, "Why would your parents be unhappy about my cat eating a rodent? That's what she is on board for. Why can't she drink milk? She loves milk. All cats do."

"Please, Mister Captain! I need to save my sister before she does something stupid. Please!" plead Sarah with the puppy-dog look and a pout to her lips.

"I don't see that what my cat eats is any concern to you or your parents, but Hannah went into the fourth door toward the aft of the ship. That way," said the captain, pointing to the rear of the boat.

Sarah said, "Thank you," as she headed in the direction that Pennywit was pointing. When she arrived at the aforementioned cabin, she slowly pushed the door open and cautiously entered the dark room. It was a small room with the only illumination coming through the open doorway. Standing there as her eyes became accustomed to the dim environment, she slowly took in the room. Dominating the dusty room was a small, unmade cot with only a lumpy mattress and pillow. Covering the cot was a frayed and thread-worn blanket. On the walls were a calendar with the date 1822 plainly visible, a few pictures, and several hooks that held rain gear and some items of clothing. In the corner was a chair.

Underneath the chair was a cat wearing a red hard hat. Hannah. She had the mouse cornered and was commencing to dab at it with her paws. The more she prodded the mouse, the more it cowered. Suddenly, Hannah recoiled as if hit by a bolt of lightning. With feet scrabbling on the wooden deck, the cat reversed out from under the chair and leapt up onto the seat. As she perched on the chair, Hannah began cleaning her paws and licking her lips.

"Oh no, Hannah!" gasped Sarah. "You didn't really eat that mouse? Did you? Tell me you didn't!"

Honk. Honk. "That means no. Actually, I chased it under the chair and was about to catch it when I remembered that I don't like mice. I didn't want to touch the mouse. Besides, I thought his little cold feet might tickle my stomach if I swallowed him. So I let him go."

"If you didn't eat the mouse, then why are you cleaning yourself?"

"Actually, that's what cats do. That's why I chased the mouse. They are always licking. I don't like it. I don't like all that hair on my tongue. Yuck!"

"Well, Hannah, we need to get out of here before something else goes wrong. Let's find a quiet place and call the phone in the arm of the chair. Then we can get home. Hannah, call the chair."

"I don't have the cell phone. I gave it to you, remember?"

"Hannah! You never gave me the phone. I don't have it. You must have it!"

"No, Sarah, I gave it to you before we got into the chair."

"No you did not!"

"Yes I did. You lost it!"

"Oh, Hannah, what are we going to do?" said Sarah on verge of tears.

CHAPTER ELEVEN

"Just kidding!" *Honk. Honk. Honk. Honk.* "I have it right here," said Hannah as she retrieved the phone. Flipping open the phone, she punched in a series of numbers, waited a few seconds, but no chair appeared. After looking around the area for the chair, the two girls looked at each other with a confused look.

Sarah said, "What did you do? Did you dial the wrong number?"

Hannah again pounded out a set of numbers. The girls waited. Nothing! Hannah began pounding on the cell phone as if that would make it operate. Hannah asked, "What can we do, Sarah? The phone doesn't work. This is all your fault. It's not my fault!"

To this, Sarah replied, "It can't be my fault because I never had the phone. We need to come up with a plan." Several seconds later, she said, "Let's get off the ship. Maybe the phone will be able to reach the chair if we get off the boat and find a deserted place. Let's try that. Okay?"

Honk. Honk. Honk. "That means yes."

As they left the cabin and proceeded along the walkway, they met Captain Pennywit standing by the gangplank. He asked, "Were you able to save Hannah?"

"Well, Hannah did not eat the mouse. She let it go. But now my sister and I need to be going home. It was nice to meet you, Mr. Pennywit. We really need to go. Thank you."

However, as the little girl and the cat started to cross the gangplank, the good captain said, "Whoa. You cannot take my cat. Hannah needs to stay here and look after the rat population. You have to leave her here."

"But…ah…but…we need to go home. Our parents will be worried."

"I'm sorry. Hannah stays here. She is needed," said the captain.

Resigned to leave her sister behind, she bent down to pet the cat. Stroking the tabby, Sarah whispered, "I can't take you off the boat. You will have to sneak off when the captain isn't looking, and I'll meet you over there behind that big tree. Okay?"

Honk. Honk. Honk. The cat meowed as she took off after another mouse.

Sarah said, "Thank you, Captain." As he waved goodbye, she wended her way down the plank, hoping that Hannah would have enough sense to not catch the mouse but head for the tree when the coast was clear. Sarah mingled her way through the excited crowd and headed for the designated tree. Because of the shoulder-to-shoulder mass of people, it was slow going. At times she had to bypass knots of spectators and other times she would duck and twist her way through them.

Arriving at the appointed tree, she immediately noticed that she was alone. No little sister. No tabby cat. Looking around for Hannah, she wondered if maybe she had caught the mouse and eaten it. *How awful!* She would be sick for days. Just about that time, she heard *honk, honk, honk, honk.* "Hi, Sarah."

Looking around for her sister was a wasted effort. Nobody or nothing was in sight. Sarah said, "Hannah, please don't play games. We need to get home so we can find you a litter box before the milk makes you sick."

"I'm fine. I didn't drink that much." *Honk.* "Here I am in the tree."

Looking up, Sarah saw her sister about seven feet up on the limb of the tree. "What are you doing up in the tree?"

"A big dog chased me up here when I was waiting for you. He almost bit my tail!"

"Well, the dog is gone now. Come down here and call the chair. I want to go home."

"I can't. I'm stuck. I'm afraid to climb down," whined Hannah.

"Oh, Hannah! Then jump. I'll catch you."

"Are you sure? Don't drop me!" With those words, she launched herself into the air and right into Sarah's waiting arms.

Holding her sister, Sarah said, "Okay, now call the chair."

Hannah flung open the phone with a practiced hand, and with a flourish, she punched in a group of numbers. Still the chair failed to appear. Looking down at the phone,

Sarah said, "Hannah! You did not turn on the phone. How can you call the chair if the phone is turned off?"

"Oh, that's why the phone doesn't work. It's not my fault," groused Hannah as she turned on the phone and keyed in some numbers. As if by magic, the chair again appeared.

As they positioned themselves in that big old chair, Hannah complained, "Sarah, my tummy hurts. Remember I'm laxatacktos intolerant."

"Yes, I know. You know that you're not supposed to drink milk. You know it will make you sick. You will just have to wait. We are going home," nagged Sarah as she typed the proper date and pushed the spacebar.

As the chair began its journey into the mouth of the plaid whale and back to the present time, Hannah again whined, "My tummy hurts. I need to potty. Real badly!"

The two girls made it back to their garage safely, and Hannah, thank goodness, made it to the bathroom in time. But Sarah was still confused as to why in all of their time travels they had not made it to the time that corresponded to what she had typed into the computer. Sarah thought about it and decided that maybe the *Grumpy* needed more power. But how do you get more power for an old chair? She would have to think on that a while. Maybe an idea would come to her later. Right now, she had other things to do.

As she had done after every adventure, she wanted to find out what they had just seen in their time travel. She commenced her research in the encyclopedia. Nothing there on Captain Pennywit or the *Robert Thompson*. She then looked in the almanac of dates for the year 1822.

Still nothing. There were quite a few history books on the shelves but nothing that would assist her in figuring out this puzzle.

Having used up all her options, she went to her mother and asked if it would be all right to fire up the computer and see what she could find online. Mom said, "Sure. Go right ahead. Do you need any help?" The reply was "No thanks. I can do it by myself. Thanks, Mom."

Seating herself at the computer table, she turned it on and proceeded to tap in the necessary keys to begin her search. Beginning with Captain Pennywit, she was inundated with a lot of information. Her only response was to pick one and begin reading and hope for the best.

- Captain Philip Pennywit was a river boat captain in the early 1800s. He was the first person to bring a riverboat up the Arkansas River to the Indian trading town of about one thousand people. The trading town was located just outside of the army post at Fort Smith, Arkansas, and would become the city of Fort Smith, Arkansas. That is why Sarah thought everything was familiar when she was wandering around the riverbank looking for her sister. It was very near to the same location as the episode with De Soto and the duel between General Pike and Governor Roane. All adventures had occurred near her own home. That explained a lot.
- From Christmas day in 1817, when Major Bradford and the sixty-four men of his command landed at Belle Point until that eventual day in 1822, the gar-

rison was provisioned by keelboat and wagon. Both were slow and provided limited supplies at the very best. However, with the arrival of the sixty-five-foot *Robert Thompson*, things changed. Not only was the *Robert Thompson* loaded down with three hundred tons of supplies, it also had two twenty-foot keelboats in tow. Yes, times did change for the better.

- However, the arrival of the first steamboat to travel up the Arkansas River is only part of the story. Captain Pennywit is just as much a part of the tale as the boat he commanded. He was to make many more runs on the river and became extremely well liked, later known as the Father of Steamboating on the Arkansas River. One of places along the river that Pennywit would make periodic landings was a small settlement called Philip's Landing where he would take on wood for fuel. The town retained the name until Martin Van Buren became post master general of the United States. At that time, the town decided to rename itself in his honor. That town is now known as Van Buren, Arkansas, and lies just across the river from Fort Smith. Pennywit would captain many more boats on the Arkansas. He retired from the river in 1841, and for a time, he operated a flour mill, mineral spa, and a riverfront warehouse downtown in Van Buren. Today he lies in Fairview Cemetery in Van Buren, Arkansas. Strangely enough, he lies not too far from the strange grave that is believed to belong to the member of De Soto's army who died and was buried in what would become Fairview Cemetery.

- Steamboats were a primary means of transporting people and cargo. In the mid 1800s, a nine-hundred-foot long dock was built at Fort Smith and was a very busy location as long as boats plied the river. The Arkansas was a demanding mistress, always holding surprises for the unsuspecting. The sandy bottom of the river was constantly changing, making navigation very tricky and, at times, lethal. In 1876, a sandbar a mile long and half-mile wide developed just below Fort Smith, creating a major obstacle. Boats had to be landed below the sandbar and passengers and freight taken into town over land.

- With the completion of the lock-and-dam system, traffic now comes and goes almost without notice. Nobody, except perhaps for small children and dreamers, gets excited about barges on the river or even a few ocean-going vessels that have cruised past Van Buren and Fort Smith.

CHAPTER TWELVE

Rainy Sunday afternoons can be boring. Cartoons were on the TV, but the girls were not paying much attention. The cartoons were mostly reruns. However, when a commercial interrupted the program, Hannah was all eyes and ears. All the ads aimed at girls would be followed by Hannah saying, "I want that! I want that! If I don't get that, I'll just die!" It did not really matter what the toy was that was being presented; they were always greeted with the same, "I want that!"

With the boredom of the afternoon and not much interest in the cartoons, there was not too much activity in the household. Every so often, a commercial would appear and Sarah would say, "I want that!" Those simple three words would provoke an argument as to who said it first and which of the girls really wanted it more. The fussing went on until finally their mother, tired of the fretting over the toy commercials, told them to turn off the TV and to go clean their room. So the TV was turned off with the moan of "Oh Mom!" and the girls trudged off to their bedroom that was waiting to be cleaned.

The girls stood just inside the bedroom door and looked at the clutter. They looked at each other. They exchanged dirty looks. Finally, Sarah said, "See. You always get me in trouble."

"I didn't do nothing. This is all your fault."

"You do too. You always start an argument. Your arguments always get me in trouble. You do it on purpose."

"I was just watching TV."

"Okay, Hannah. Let's get to work and clean up this mess," glowered Sarah. She began throwing toys, clothes, books, anything that was on the floor into the closet.

Hannah walked over to her Scooby-Do haunted house and began playing.

"Quit playing and get to work." demanded Sarah.

"You're not the boss of me. You can't tell me what to do."

"Hannah! We need to get this room cleaned up before Mom gripes us out again!"

"I don't care."

"Well I do!" said Sarah as she walked over, picked up the play house and put it on the toy shelf.

"That's mine." wailed Hannah.

"We need to clean the room."

"I don't care. I want to play."

Just then their mother appeared in the doorway. "What's with all the squabbling? I told you to clean this room. Now stop the arguing and get busy. I don't want to have to tell you again. Now get busy."

As their mother left Sarah whispered, "See. You got me in trouble again."

"I didn't do nothing. You put away the toy I was playing with. Leave my stuff alone."

Sarah put away some of her dolls and then picked up Hannah's unicorn. This was met with, "AAAhh. That's mine. Leave my stuff alone!" She grabbed the unicorn from Sarah's hand. Next she started to toss Sarah's toys and clothing onto Sarah's bed.

"What are you doing? We need to clean the room."

"That's your side of the room. You have to stay on your side. Don't come on to my side." She then proceeded to draw an imaginary line down the middle of the room.

"But Hannah, the closet is on your side of the room. How can I put my stuff away?"

"I don't know and I don't care. Stay on your side."

"Okay, Hannah, if that's the way you want it. You have to stay on your half of the room. Just remember that the door is on my side. You can't come on my side. You can't get out of the room. You will just have to stay there. When you have to go to the bathroom, just remember."

"You can't do that. That's not fair."

"It was your idea."

Hannah looked at her big sister for a while and then said, "Let's be friends. We need to clean the room."

So the girls once more in harmony began to clean the room. Before long, with the room only partially cleaned and the closet so crammed full of "stuff" that it took both girls to shut the door, the girls fell into normal play with all newly rediscovered toys that had not seen daylight for some time.

Before long, the girls were once again making plans to board the *Grumpy* and continue their quest for more adventures. Suiting up in their vortex uniforms took some effort. Because now that their room was cleaned up, the different parts of the uniforms were stuffed in various part of the room. Some of the items were crammed in dressers. Other parts had been tossed into the toy chest. There at the bottom of the closet, underneath the clutter, were other selected items of apparel. In other words, the once partially clean room became a tangled landscape with hazards to the unwary traveler.

Attired in their time travel uniforms, they now had to decide where to go in history. After much haranguing, the selection was made; and the two courageous explorers headed to the garage to board their time machine. As they passed through the living room, they bid their mother adieu and entered the hangar to board the *Grumpy*.

Climbing into the chair, they arranged themselves in their respective stations and made preparations for the mission. Sarah had decided that a visit to the Pilgrims landing at Plymouth Rock would be an interesting afternoon. They could observe their hardships and watch as the brave settlers began to make a new start to their lives. As Sarah typed 1620 into the keyboard, Hannah was busy pushing her red hard hat up off her right ear. In between shoving the hat back to where it belonged, she was going through the preflight checklist on her clipboard. As always, she carefully marked off each item on the list.

When all the items on the list had been covered, she laid the clipboard and pencil down and looked over at sister. Sarah was busy checking all the connections of the controls. Remembering the last adventure's false start, she reached into the arm of the chair, pulled out the clock, and proceeded to wind it. As Sarah was taking care of business, Hannah was taking care of her own business. With her sister preoccupied with the clock, Hannah, with stealth and precision, slowly inched her hand over the keyboard and quietly typed in the numbers 1858. There was no reason for changing the date. It was done purely to aggravate her sister. Hannah, like most younger siblings, had an advanced degree in irritating her older sister. It just came naturally, with no rhyme or reason.

With all the preparations completed, Sarah said, "Hannah, are you ready?"

Reaching up to the horn, Hannah said, "Sure." *Honk. Honk. Honk.* "That means yes."

The girls were not intimidated by the action of the chair or their surroundings of the garage as the time vortex took hold of the chair. The lights flared and flickered. The humming started. The walls began puckering and spinning. It was all commonplace to them. The droning in their ears became louder. The chair began to shake and shudder. The plaid whale opened its gaping maw to receive the travelers, and the chair began its backward movement into the total darkness. The chair began to bounce like a pogo stick when Sarah heard little sister say, "Oh poop!" Then all was quiet, dark, and calm.

CHAPTER THIRTEEN

As Sarah sat in the darkness, she knew that Hannah was not with her. Hannah had done it again. She was gone. Why couldn't she stay in the chair? Now Sarah was going to have to go looking for her again. Sitting in the dark confined space, she thought she heard a strange noise. It sounded like horses galloping. Still not able to see through the surrounding blackness, the clopping became louder, and she became aware of a bumping, swaying motion like a spoonful of Jell-O sliding down a washboard. As the dark shadows began to lift, she became aware of the swirling dust that had begun to smother and choke her. The gloom combined with the heat, the swaying motion, and the dust was enough to make most people sick. Sarah wasn't feeling too well.

With the lifting of the darkened shroud that had encased the chair, she was able to take in her new environment. Sarah was in, of all places, a small wooden box that was bouncing and swaying to the point that she was having trouble keeping in her seat. Inside the box were three men across from her and a middle-aged woman sitting on the bench beside her. There was one noticeable absence. Hannah! Looking at the woman sitting next to her, Sarah noticed that she was dressed in a long, full dress. On her head was a bonnet that was tied snuggly under her chin and a parasol laying across her lap. In a voice that was hampered by the dust that churned around her, Sarah asked the woman, "Have you seen my little sister? I seem to have misplaced her. Can you help me?"

"Why, no dear. You are the only girl I've seen. When did you lose her?" responded the woman through gritty teeth.

"I lost her just a few minutes ago. I must find her or my mother will be very upset. She is only five years old."

"Are you all right dear? How could I see your sister? We left Memphis, Tennessee, two days ago. There are just the five of us. There has been no one else in the coach. Did you lose your sister before we left?"

Sarah was really beginning to get worried. She said, "No, ma'am. I just now lost her. She was with me until just a few minutes ago. You must have seen her!"

"You must have had a bad dream. Are you feeling sick? All this rocking and swaying can make a person sick if they are not careful. Do you need something to drink? Here, take a sip of this cool water. It will make you feel better," soothed the woman as she handed Sarah a bottle of water.

As Sarah took the offered water bottle, she had a lump in her throat and had moved from merely worried to panicked. Taking a sip of water, her thoughts turned to her "fuzz-brained," "lunk-headed" sister. She thought, *Why can she not stay put? Why is she always causing me so much trouble?*

What could she do to find her sister? Maybe she should get off the stage now and go back to find Hannah while she could. *Oh no… Hannah has the cell phone. How am I going to call the chair? This is not good!*

How could she get back to tell her parents that she had lost her sister while taking a ride on a stagecoach? The situation was getting worse all the time.

Sarah said to the woman sitting next to her, "I need to get off! I have to go back to find my sister! Stop the stage!"

The woman looked down at Sarah as if she was a babbling idiot. With care and comfort in her voice, she stated, "Oh no, young lady! We can't stop the stage, and you can't go back looking for her. There is nothing behind us except wilderness. You had best go to the next stop. Then you can get the next stage back to your home and look for your sister. Everything will be all right. You'll see."

Sarah took another sip of water to keep the panic out of her voice. She asked, "How long before our next stop?"

"We should make Fort Smith sometime late tonight."

"Fort Smith? You mean Fort Smith, Arkansas?"

"That's right dear, Fort Smith, Arkansas. It won't be much longer."

Sarah thought, *Maybe it is for the best if I ride the stage into the next stop. At least I would be close to where I started from. Maybe something will happen. Maybe Hannah will be waiting for me. Why is Hannah always causing me trouble?*

The dusty, uncomfortable, bouncing ride took forever to arrive in Fort Smith. Sarah napped when she could, but her coughing and the larger bumps would wake her with a start. Maybe it was best not to sleep because she kept dreaming of her lost sister and how finally she would have the entire bedroom all to herself.

"Hannah! Turn the radio down. I'm trying to sleep," complained Sarah. The radio was so loud that she was unable to sleep. Waking up, she realized it wasn't the radio. Over the hoofbeat of the horses she could hear music. It was a band playing. There were people shouting. Some were discharging their weapons into the air. It was as if the world had gone mad.

The man—wearing a long linen duster, broad-brimmed, flat-crowned hat, and boots—who was sitting on the bench across from Sarah pulled a gold watch and long chain from his vest pocket. He flipped open the cover and said, "10:30 p.m. We made it right on time."

Suddenly the stagecoach came to a halt, but the dust continued to swirl around the air as it entered the coach through the open windows. Looking out the window, she noticed a band and a group of men on horses. She asked the adults, "Is it a hold up? Are bad men going to rob us?"

The woman took Sarah's hand and said, "It doesn't look like a robbery. I've never heard of robbers who had a band playing background music. I think we will be okay."

After a short deliberation between the stagecoach driver and a few of the riders from the escort, everything began to move. The band led the way followed by the coach. Bringing up the rear, the sides, and anywhere they wanted to be were the riders. Everyone was whooping and shouting. Guns were going off, and the band was blaring.

Before long, the coach lurched to a stop. If it was possible, the noise outside became louder. As Sarah peered out the window, she noticed that there was another stage-coach, exactly like the one she was riding in, just off to her right. After a short conversation between the driver of the two coaches and several of the riders, the procession again began to move, accompanied by the band and the noisy, excited followers who continued to grow by the minute. Sarah wished that Hannah was there because she always enjoyed a parade. *What happened to Hannah? Where could she be? I hope she's all right*, Sarah thought worriedly.

When the buildings of a town appeared, the gentleman in the duster and flat-brimmed hat again pulled out his gold watch and announced the time as 2:00 a.m. With a knowing look on his face, he closed the cover and returned it to his vest pocket. Sarah thought, with a small grin on her face, that maybe with his interest in the time he might also be a time traveler. She hoped that he hadn't lost his little brother.

The two stagecoaches pulled up and stopped in front of a wooden building. As the tired travelers climbed down from the coach with stiff joints and covered in a fine dust from their travels, the assembled crowd grew louder and larger. The windows of businesses and homes glowed with newly lit candles and lanterns. Whistles were blown, guns fired, bells were rung, and a cannon from the fort was touched off. A leather pouch was carried into the building that sported a sign that read "City Hall."

Sarah looked back at the dusty stagecoach and read the name lettered on the side. It read "Butterfield Overland Stage Line." At least now she knew what she had been riding in. She witnessed the growing multitude and the increasing noise with amazement. What was going on? Why was everyone celebrating at this time in the morning? She wondered who she could find who would help her locate her sister and the cell phone. Asking the people scurrying past did no good. Everyone was more concerned with the celebration than with helping her locate her lost sister.

Giving up, at least for now, she sat down (*honk*) on the wooden steps beside the coach and put her chin in her cupped hands (*honk*) to wait. Maybe things would be (*honk*) better when the sun was (*honk*) shining. Suddenly, she started. Did she just hear that (*honk*) bike horn? Yes! There it was again. *Honk. Honk. Honk.* "What's the matter, Sarah? Did you miss me?" *Honk. Honk.*

Sarah jumped up and looked around. Her eyes wide and alert even though it was late, and she scanned every face in the crowd. No Hannah in sight. "Hannah, where are you?" questioned Sarah.

"Right here, silly! I'm right in front of you." *Honk. Honk.*

Looking right in front of her, all she saw was the stagecoach and the horses. Upon taking a closer look, she noticed that the lead horse harnessed to the coach was wearing a red hard hat with horn and flashlight attached. Walking over to the horse she said, "Hannah, is that you? What are you doing as a horse?"

"I don't know. When we hit that big bump, I was bumped out of the chair. Then I was running with these other horses. I like being a horse, but it's not fun pulling this wagon."

"Why can't you stay with me? Do you always have to get lost? I was very worried," Sarah lectured as she wagged her finger at the horse.

"It wasn't my fault. You are the one who didn't put the seat belts on the chair. If it had seat belts, I would not have been bumped out of the chair. I was just sitting there. I wasn't doing anything. It's all your fault. Not mine. Where are we?"

"We are in Fort Smith," said Sarah.

"Actually, it doesn't look like Fort Smith. Not at all."

"Oh, Hannah. This is the way Fort Smith looked five hundred years ago." Sarah looked up and saw the woman from the coach standing by watching Sarah lecture the horse.

"Dear," said the woman, "are you all right? Can I do anything to help? Do you need to sit down? Do I need to get a doctor?"

"Oh no, ma'am. Thank you. I'm just talking to my sister."

"Your sister? That looks like a horse. Is your sister a horse?"

"Did I say sister? I meant I'm just talking to this nice horse."

"If you need help, you just let me know." Shaking her head, the woman walked away, convinced that Sarah needed a full-time keeper.

Sarah turned to the horse with the red hard hat and said, "See. You've done it to me again. You always get me into trouble."

"I didn't do nothing. I was just standing here. It's not my fault."

"Oh, Hannah."

About that time, some men came leading another set of horses. They unhitched Hannah and the other horses from the stagecoach and hitched the new team to the coach. They then led the tired horses, including Hannah, away. Sarah had no option but to follow and see where they were taking her sister.

A few short blocks away, the horses were ushered into a stable where they were to be fed, watered, and bedded down for the night. Sarah lingered outside the stable until the men were done tending to the team and left. As she entered the building, she wondered how she would be able to locate her sister. This turned out to be easier than she thought. All she had to do was look for the hard had perched on top of one of the horses' heads.

There in the corner Sarah saw the red hat. Approaching the hat, she noticed that Hannah was eating hay. *That can't taste very good.* "How do you like being a horse?" she asked.

"Well, actually, it's not as much fun as I thought. I don't get to run and play. Pulling that wagon is hard work and the food is awful."

"What do you say we get out of here?" asked Sarah. "I've had enough history for one night."

"Sure. I'm ready for some egg yolk and toast. I also want a Coke. Let's go home," said Hannah. So she pulled out the cell phone and tapped in random numbers and, as if by magic, the chair appeared.

Sarah slid into the chair easily and began to enter the correct date in the computer. While she was doing this, Hannah was trying to arrange herself in the time machine. This was easier said than done. Chairs are not made to accommodate horses. It took a little wiggling and a lot of squirming, but she somehow managed to fit herself into the chair.

"Are you ready?" asked Sarah.

Honk. Honk. Honk. "That means yes."

And so the pair began their journey back to the current point on the timeline of the space continuum. As with all time travel, they arrived back home at the exact same time as their departure from home. Hannah once again returned home as a little girl and not as a horse. This was just as well because her mother would not have allowed her in the house, and she would have had to sleep in the garage and eat hay and not have any Coke to drink. That would not do.

Another adventure was completed. Now it was time to discover what they had just witnessed. An adventure in time now called for an adventure on the ethereal highway known as the Internet. Sarah lit up the computer and entered "Butterfield Overland Stage Line" and waited for the result.

- For starters, Sarah was wrong. It was not Fort Smith of five hundred years ago. The date was September 19, 1858, when the Butterfield stage entered the town of less than three thousand people. At that time, there was no bank in the town, and for that matter, there was not even any printed currency in use. What made this small Indian trading town become the most important point on the overland mail route? It was the junction of the mail line. The stage that Hannah was pulling came from Memphis, Tennessee, and was joined by the stage that began in St. Louis, Missouri. The leather pouch that was carried into the court house was 7 ¾ pounds of mail that was taken in to be sorted.

- The coach that arrived from California caused even more excitement. All the businesses were closed, and the town decorated to properly celebrate the link to the outside world. A parade was decided upon with decorated wagons and floats, a marching band, city firemen, a unit from the army post, and even a passing circus was conscripted. Just as Santa follows Christmas parades, John Butterfield in his finest Concord Coach rounded out the procession. Ceremonies were held on the government reservation, and of course, all the local dignitaries gave speeches. The day's activities ended with a gala ball and banquet.

- The Concord coach was chosen because of its style, size, and sturdiness. The rough roads, mountains, and river crossings required a dependable vehicle. The coach could carry up to nine passengers. Each person was allowed up to forty pounds of baggage. The average rate of travel was about 120 miles per day. For safety reasons, no shipments of gold or silver were carried by the coaches. Stations were anywhere from ten to twenty miles apart, and two meals were served Depending on the type of meal, the cost was from forty cents to a dollar per person. The cost of the coach ride was $150 for each passenger and it was the same whether the rider was going east or west.

- The section of the route that ran from St. Louis to Fort Smith came through Van Buren, Arkansas, down what was basically Log Town Hill (HWY 59), past Park View Cemetery (where Captain Pennywit and the lost conquistador are buried) to Main Street where the stage was either ferried across the Arkansas River during high water or forded when the river was low. Low water was dangerous because of the quicksand and the weight of the loaded coach. From the ferry, it was only about six miles into Fort Smith.

- The man in the duster and hat who kept looking at his watch was John Butterfield. He had taken the mail pouch and began the trip from St. Louis. He caused quite a stir with his attire, and in fact, it became a fashion style for young men for many years to come. His stage line only lasted until 1871 when the telegraph and the transcontinental railroad drew the last of his passengers and cargo. It may be part of our colorful past, but the words of John Butterfield to his employees will remain in history: "Remember, boys, nothing on God's earth must stop the United States Mail."

CHAPTER FOURTEEN

As happens with most children, Hannah had to make her twice a year visit to the dentist's chair. It was only to be a cleaning and checkup. Well, it turned out that Grumpy had too much of an influence on her early years. Too much soda. Grumpy had always said, "Coke has two of the major food groups: caffeine and sugar. What else is needed?" The checkup required further visits to fill several small cavities in her young mouth. Or as the dentist put it, "You have several small 'cavity bugs' on your teeth. What we will do is put some stars on the bugs. That will take care of it. Does that sound okay?" However, this was Hannah's first fillings. No one had any idea of the drama that was about to play out. She had no idea of what to expect. Neither her mother, the dentist, nor anyone within the sound of a sonic boom had any idea of the sideshow to come.

The first visit went well. Teeth cleaned and x-rays. No problem. The first follow-up excursion to the dentist was a nightmare for Hannah, her mother, the dentist, Sarah, and the all the patients in the waiting room.

The dentist did the normal dentist thing. "Open wide please." He examined her teeth, checked the best x-rays he had ever seen, pronounced himself ready, and commenced with his duties. The injection went okay to numb her teeth. No big problem, but the circus was about to start. It was when the drilling procedures began that the difficulties were first noted. The more he drilled, the more Hannah began to howl and squirm. As the squirming and screams became more pronounced, the dentist asked, "Oh. Does that hurt?"

Hannah gave a definite, "YES! IT HURTS!" and closed her mouth tightly until her lips disappeared.

The dentist said, "Well, we'll just have to deaden it some more." He then picked up his hypo, peeled Hannah's lip upward, and injected some more nerve killer. Hannah did not feel the injection. She drooled. "Mom, my mouth feels funny."

Pausing shortly for the additional numbing to take effect, he again began to ply his trade. Numbed or not, Hannah was not having any part of this fiasco. The more the drill whined, the deeper she dug herself into the chair. The tears commenced, the yelling mingled with the buzzing of the drill, and Hannah began to kick and wave her arms to ward off this assault of her oral cavity.

The hijinks in the reclined chair became so pronounced that her mom tried to hold Hannah still while the dentist drilled. There was only one mom and one small little girl with six arms and six legs swirling around the chair like an octopus on steroids sitting on a runaway jackhammer. Her mom ended up sitting on Hannah to hold her down. But it wasn't enough. Before long, the dental assistant was brought into the act to help hold her down. This only made things worse. They thought they were going to need to ask Sarah and the some of the patients in the waiting room for assistance. As the call for help went out, the dentist decided he had either drilled enough or he just plain ran out of patience and removed the drill from her mouth. This simple act quieted Hannah down enough that her mom could keep her confined to the chair for the duration of the procedure.

All of this commotion in the other room had Sarah on edge. It disturbed her quite a bit. She had never witnessed such a demonstration in her life! It wasn't enough for her to go see a skull farmer, but she would need a lot of quiet time for her nerves to settle.

The dentist made Hannah's next appointment with another dentist.

The family arrived home more or less as they had left. Hannah slept for several hours, snorting and sniveling while asleep. But she woke up and was ready to go. Their homework was done and supper was not quite ready. What could they do? As usual, Sarah took the lead and said, "Let's do something fun! We can go back in time and be home before supper is ready. How does that sound, Hannah?"

"I wish I had been a rabbit at the dentist's office. That way I could have run away and nobody could catch me. I think it would be nice to be a rabbit. I am not going anywhere in that chair until you fix it. You need to put on some seat belts! Every time we go someplace I get bounced out. Last time I was a horse. A horse was okay, but I had to pull that wagon, got all dusty, slept in a barn, and ate dried grass. That wasn't any fun. I am not going."

"Hannah, that's a good idea. We can fix seat belts in the *Grumpy* while we wait for supper to get ready. First, we have to find something that we can use for seat belts."

"I got a good idea," exclaimed Hannah as she dashed off into her parent's bedroom. Moments later, she reappeared carrying two of her dad's belts. "We can buckle these around our waists, and they will hold us in the chair. Isn't that a good idea?"

"It's a good idea to hold up our pants, but how do we fasten the belts to the chair? Besides, Dad may want his belts to keep his pants up. We don't want his pants to fall down when he is coaching the basketball team. That would be awful. Besides, the belts are not long enough to go around the chair."

Hannah snickered. "No, that would be funny if he stood up and his pants fell down… hee, hee, hee."

"No, it would not be funny. It would be bad. Now what else can we use? Let's think."

"Maybe we could use the car seats from Mom's car," said Hannah. "That would keep us safe."

"Two things," replied Sarah. "First, Mom would not let us take them from the car."

"Maybe she wouldn't notice they were gone," interrupted Hannah.

"Mom would know, and then I would get in trouble. Second, how do we fasten the seats to the chair? If the seats are not fastened to the chair, they won't keep us safe. We need a better idea. Think!"

Both girls thought for a few moments. Finally, Hannah's face lit up. Holding up her right hand beside her face, index finger extended toward the ceiling, she said, "I know. I got a great idea. We could use tape."

"Hannah, we are out of tape. You used the last of it when you taped the flashlight to the hard hat. But that gives me an idea. We could tie ourselves into the chair by using the twine that's left. That's a great idea. Let's go see how it works," said Sarah as she headed out to the garage and the waiting time machine.

Hannah followed her sister out to the garage. But the whole time she complained, "My ideas were good. Sarah just didn't want to use them because I thought of them first. If she had thought of the ideas they would have been good ideas. Because I thought of them they weren't good. She's always the boss. When can I be boss?"

As they entered the garage, Hannah was still protesting. Digging around in the pile of stuff that was liberated from Grumpy's garage, Sarah soon emerged with the ball of twine. Looking up, she asked Hannah if she knew where the scissors were.

To the question, Hannah pouted and said, "I don't know. Maybe Bigfoot took them."

"Hannah, if you find them, you can cut the rope. How does that sound?"

"Okay. If I find the scissors, I get to cut," exclaimed Hannah as she walked over to the shelves on the back wall of the garage. There, where she had hidden them behind several cans of paint, were the missing shears. With a grin of her face, she returned to the chair, scissors in hand, and said in a singsong voice, "I found them so I get to use them."

"Hannah, you hid them. Why did you hide them? That's not fair."

"I just didn't want them to get lost."

Having dealt with similar situations before, Sarah saw no point in arguing. She simply held out the twine for her sister to cut. Of course, when they tried it, the first length of twine was too short. "Look, Hannah. You cut it too short. Why did you make it so short? It won't work," scolded Sarah.

"It wasn't my fault. You held the rope. It was your fault. You made me cut it too short. Don't blame me," retorted Hannah.

Just about that time the door to the kitchen opened, and their mom said that supper would be a little late. Because they had work to do, they didn't really care. They returned back to the necessary repairs to the time machine. This time, playing out more rope, Sarah said, "Cut right here. Don't make this one too short."

"It was your fault, not mine. You held the rope."

"Hannah, just cut the twine," bossed Sarah.

"Okay. Okay," carped Hannah as she snipped the twine at the point Sarah indicated.

Taking the scissors from her sister, Sarah played out more twine and cut a section for herself. Then she said, "Ready to put on our traveling uniforms and enter the curtain of time. Are you ready, Hannah?"

"I guess so. You didn't let me cut your rope. Why did you not let me cut it? I wouldn't have made it too short."

"Never mind, Hannah. Let's get ready. This will be fun."

"Okay. But next time I get to cut," demanded Hannah, as the two brave vortex warriors left the garage for their bedroom to don their uniforms.

With only minor bickering, they emerged back into the vortex laboratory ready to battle the maelstrom of time. They were attired much as on their other adventures. Hannah's red hard hat still insisted on sliding down until its movements were arrested by her right ear. Headgear, gloves, goggles, and bare feet…they were ready for anything.

Climbing into the chair, careful to avoid all the added equipment, they began the start-up procedures. Sarah began her "walk around inspection" just like all good pilots. She double-checked all the connections and made sure the clock was wound. While she was doing her pilot's check, Hannah was going through the start-up checklist.

"Helmets? Check."

"Goggles? Check."

"Headphones? Check."

"Gloves? Check."

"Horn? Check."

"Flashlight? Check."

"Seat belts? Check. Sarah, we need to fasten out seat belts."

Both girls looped the rope around the chair and fastened it around their waists. At least Sarah did. Hannah was having trouble tying the ends together. She still had trouble tying the laces on her shoes. Hannah wound the ends of the rope around each other, making loops around her fingers, tucking one end here and the other there. Nothing worked. Finally, she had to ask her sister for help. Being the kindly older sister, Sarah reached over and unraveled the mess in Hannah's lap and tied a perfect bow. Now they were all set except for one small problem. Where to go?

"Where would you like to go?" Sarah asked. "I always pick the place, and we never seem to go to the right time. Today you get to pick."

"I don't care, Sarah. You pick."

"No, Hannah. You get to pick."

"But I don't know."

"Come on, Hannah. You pick. Just enter a time and we will go there. Okay?"

Honk, Honk. Honk. "That means yes," honked Hannah listlessly as she leaned over and typed the date 1817. No reason. Not even paying any attention to the keys as she typed. "Okay. Ready, Sarah?"

Sarah reached over and squeezed the bulb on the horn on Hannah's head. *Honk. Honk. Honk.* "That means yes."

"Don't honk my horn, Sarah. It's my horn."

Even as she fussed about Sarah honking her horn, she pressed the proper key on the computer and the game was afoot.

The garage went through all of its shenanigans, and before long, the black-and-white plaid whale opened its gaping mouth and swallowed the adventurers.

Not knowing where they were going, what they would witness, or even when they were heading, Sarah only knew that it was going to be a trip to remember. Suddenly, as if on cue, the chair hit one of the many columns in the space and time continuum. As the chair bumped and skewed sideways, she heard Hannah say, "Oh NO. Not again!" Once again, there was only complete silence and total blackness.

CHAPTER FIFTEEN

Once again, Sarah found herself alone in the darkness. Hannah appeared to be missing again! The silence was total and the darkness completely enveloped her. She sat and waited for a few minutes while her brain fine-tuned itself from the stresses of traveling at light speed through the maze of time. As had happened in the past, the gods of time began to slowly remove their hands from Sarah's eyes and ears. At first she became aware of a gentle rocking motion. Before too much time had passed, her hearing picked up the rippling and splashing noise of a fairly large mass of water. Finally, the fog of darkness began to lift, revealing a chilly landscape.

There was enough chill in the air that the water in the calmer areas, inlets, and backwaters was beginning glaze over in a layer of ice. The ice was not thick enough to support anything larger than a chipmunk. It was not more than the thickness of a thin pane of opaque glass that would splinter at the footfall of any large animal that tried to tread on the slick surface. Jack Frost sponsored the redecoration of the countryside by swooping down the valleys and the flat lands with his monochromatic pallet and painted the scenery like a whitewashed fence.

As her vision cleared, the first thing that was apparent was—no Hannah. Lost, just like always. Once again, Sarah was going to have to find her sister. Giving her surroundings a quick glance, she noticed that she was on a boat about fifty or sixty feet long. It looked strangely familiar. She had seen one before. Suddenly she remembered. It looked a lot like the keelboats that Captain Pennywit had pulled behind his steamship. She must be on a keelboat! But why was she here and what was happening?

Continuing her visual tour of the surroundings, she noticed that there were two keelboats both headed in the same direction, upriver. The boats were loaded with supplies and about thirty or thirty-five men on each boat. The men were dressed in white trousers and fancy gray uniforms with enough silver buttons and piping to outfit a marching band. On their heads were tall blue felt hats with matching braid and a small white plume. The uniforms looked a lot like the ones she had seen on West Point Cadets in pictures and TV. Judging from the uniforms and the long wooden and steel rifles stored nearby, Sarah deduced that they must be soldiers. But who were they? Where were they going? Did the rifles mean danger?

The soldiers were busy with long poles. They would put the poles in the water at the front of the boats until the poles would hit the river bottom and then, while pushing on the poles, walk to the rear of the boat. Arriving at the back of the boat, they would pull the poles out of the water and walk back to the front and repeat the process again and again. Pushing the boats against the strong current was a difficult and slow procedure. It took a lot of muscle and stamina, not to mention a few groans and an occasional oath muttered under their breath.

One man stood at the rear of the boat with a wooden bar grasped in his rough and calloused hands. The bar was connected to the rudder. He was able to control the movement of the keelboat by swinging the bar in the opposite direction that he wanted to steer. Located at the front was another soldier who was carefully watching for sandbars, snags, floating logs, or anything else that might strike and damage the boat.

Those men who were not in the act of poling the keelboats were busy tending to equipment and provisions. Some men were cleaning rifles, cleaning personal equipment, checking to be sure the provisions were secured, and several appeared to be standing guard, as if waiting for some misfortune that was about to fall. Interspersed among all the men were several black men in uniform. They were as busy at work as all the rest of the troops.

On each keelboat were two women. The women were dressed in long full dresses that reached to their ankles. On their heads were bonnets attached by ribbons cinched tightly under their chin. They were located more toward the center of the boat, and they seemed to be doing more mundane projects like mending clothing, doing laundry, or preparing the food for the next meal. Some of the men appeared to be sick, and someone was constantly tending to their needs. Everyone on the boats appeared busy and hard at work. This did not look like a place for slackers. Everyone pulled their weight.

As she continued her observations, Sarah noticed that in the center of the boat was a man who stood out from the rest of the soldiers. His head was bowed, and he was leaning over a barrel that acted like his desk. He was sorting through and writing on papers and what appeared to be a logbook. What made him stand out was not what he was doing, but how he was dressed. He was impeccably attired. His uniform was more elaborate and sported a lot more gold braid. On his shoulders appeared to be gold brushes. Around his neck was a silken scarf. The cuffs of his tunic were covered with layers of gold braid. Sitting on a barrel beside him was his hat. The hat is what caught Sarah's eye. It was different than any she had seen before. It was narrow from front to back. When he placed it upon his head, it reminded Sarah of a Viking ship with the high contoured front and aft with the raised center like the single sail on the ship.

Unable to locate her sister, Sarah decided that she would ask the man with the hat if he had seen her or knew her whereabouts. "Mr. Hat" seemed to be the one in charge. As she approached the tall man in the gold braids, she heard the man from the front of the boat yell, "Major Bradford, we are coming upon a fork in the river. Which way do we need to steer?"

The major's reply was "We'll take the larger of the two forks. Stay in the main channel. Maybe Major Long will have left a marker for us to follow. We should know when we get closer to the division of the two rivers."

"Yes, sir," came the reply from the man at the rudder as he maintained their position in the river.

As the two keelboats came around the bend in the river and approached the union of the two rivers, they heard rifle shots. The soldier in the front of the lead boat yelled back to the major, "Sir, there are gunshots and campfires to port. There are two men on the bluff. They are waving at us. They seem to want to get our attention."

"I believe those are two of the men we sent in the advanced party with Major Long," said Major Bradford as he pointed his spyglass in their direction. "Steer in their direction. I believe we have arrived at our future home."

As the boats fought the powerful currents of the collective rivers, trying to attain the rocky bank and steep crags of the riverbank, Sarah approached the major. She wanted to find out if anybody had seen Hannah. Up close, the major was a nice-looking man, but his expression was stern, almost severe. The closer Sarah got to him, the more her courage failed. Just as she was about to change her mind and retreat to the "safety" of two women, he looked up from his papers and said, "What do you want, young lady? I'm very busy right now. It had better be important. What is it you want?"

Sarah looked into his unyielding eyes and could only stammer and stutter. The words failed to complete their journey from her head to her tongue and remained sealed away in her brain. Nothing would leave her mouth except gibberish. At long last, she blurted out the words, "Excuse me, sir. I have lost my little sister. Have you seen a little girl of about five years old?"

"No. It will have to wait. We'll look for her later. Right now, we have to get across this swift current and find out what awaits on shore. Now is not the time."

With a sigh of relief, she was happy to be out from under the commanding presence and away from those icy, Spartan eyes. Sarah would continue her search for Hannah from the safety of the far end of the boat.

Surviving their crosscurrent journey, the two boats, amid rifle shots and whoops and hollers, safely arrived on the rocky riverbank below the towering heights. They beached their keelboats onto a rock-layered landing site that was situated just below the tall, imposing bluffs. As Major Bradford stepped ashore, he was met by the two men who had hailed the boats. They saluted the major and greeted him with, "Welcome to Belle Point. Major Long said this was the ideal site to erect the fort. He named it Camp Smith. Here are the plans for the fort that he drew up. He bought some horses and took the rest of the men to explore and survey the area."

Major Bradford quickly surveyed the location and agreed with Major Long that this was the best site for a military outpost. The first order of business for the soldiers was to establish camp, unload the keelboats, prepare meals, and place sentries at selected intervals. The ensuing days would involve a lot of toil and labor. The land had to be cleared of trees and stumps, stones moved, stockade walls erected, and buildings established. Some troops would have to clear land for the planting of crops. Here at this desolate outpost, the fort would have to be self-sufficient for almost all their needs.

With all the activity around her, Sarah once again began her search for her errant sister. She began by looking over, in, and on both keelboats. No Hannah. Next she began to check all the crates and assorted stores that had been unloaded from the boats. Still, no Hannah.

Honk. Honk. Honk. "Over here, Sarah. Here I am."

Following the honking like a bird dog on the trail of a covey of quail, Sarah followed the honking until she found the red hard hat in some bushes that encircled a small grove of trees. Beneath the hard hat stood a tan rabbit grinning large enough to see the cap on one of the teeth. The long ears kept the hat perched in the center of the rabbit's head. Sarah thought it was the cutest thing she had ever seen and stooped to pick up the furry critter.

"I am so happy to see you, Hannah. What happened to you this time?"

"I don't know. All of a sudden it was dark and when the lights came back on, I saw you getting off the boat. Where are we, Sarah?" replied Hannah.

"I don't know, but it does seem familiar. Let's look around. Maybe we can find out. There were a bunch of busy people aboard the boat. They seemed to know where they were going. Maybe we can find out. Let's look over there," whispered Sarah as she began stroking the furry bundle with the red hat.

"Ahhhhhh. That feels good," said Hannah as she relaxed in her big sister's arms. She laid her long ears back, which caused the red hard hat to shift about on her head and tried to slide off. Sarah righted the hat and kept stroking the soft fur as she began to walk around.

Stopping at the keelboats, she watched as several of the men began to organize, sort, and catalogue all the supplies that had been unloaded. Several men approached the assembled supplies, and they were issued a pile of canvas, poles, and ropes. They were also given instructions of where to set up camp and how the tents were to be arranged.

No sooner had that group of soldiers left with their tents to set up camp when another group appeared. This detachment of soldiers was given axes, saws, shovels, and picks. Part of the group was instructed to start clearing the land, removing the stump and rocks. They were to prepare the land for plowing and planting. The crops would be required to supplement their food supplies later in the year. The rest of the men were ordered to report to Major Bradford to begin construction of the fort that was laid out by Major Long. Sarah and Hannah stood there for a while watching the activity, but before long, Hannah said, "Let's go look at something else. I want to do something that's fun."

Passing around the side of one of the keelboats, she noticed a small group of people standing on the far side of the river. Taking a closer look, Sarah's eyes widened, her mouth gaped open, revealing her silver braces, and she stopped dead in her tracks. There just across the river were four men. What set them apart was their appearance. The dark-skinned men were wrapped in heavy robes, with bare legs and what looked like moccasins on their feet. The moccasins appeared to be stuffed with grass as insulation against the cold weather. Their hair was festooned with feathers and long strips of what looked like fur. Each man carried a weapon. Three of the men clutched short bows and on their backs were quivers that contained extra arrows. The other man held a spear. The serious countenance on their faces did not look overly friendly.

Her long ears stood up, causing the hard hat to shift, and the pink nose began to twitch. "Who are they? What do they want? We need to get out of here!" fretted Hannah.

CHAPTER SIXTEEN

As she settled the hard hat back into place between Hannah's long ears, Sarah said, "I don't know for sure, but they look like Indians. Maybe we need to tell somebody that they are over there. Maybe Major Bradford will know what to do."

In a hurried pace, Sarah, with Hannah held tightly in her arms, began looking for Major Bradford. After a few panic-filled moments, they found the major with a group of soldiers working on top of the bluff. There located at the summit of the steep overlook to the junction of the two rivers, work was proceeding at a rapid pace. The men under the major's watchful eye and practiced understanding were in the process of cutting trees, shaping them, and creating long wooden walls. Major Bradford was holding what looked like plans and was directing the creation of the fort atop the riverbank.

With trepidation, the two girls—well, make that a young girl and a furry rabbit—approached the major and the small group of men who were quite intent on a discussion of the best ways to follow the plans. As she waited for the best opportunity to break into the men's conversation, Sarah began to stroke the rabbit faster and faster, harder and harder. Finally, Hannah said, "Sarah! Not so hard. You will wear all of my hair." *Honk. Honk. Honk.*

Sarah was about to apologize to the rabbit in her arms when the major looked up with his stern, penetrating eyes and asked the youngster standing in front of him, "What is so pressing that you have to interrupt our important work?"

This intimidated Sarah so much that she couldn't put into words to what she wanted to say. "Come, come," said the major, "speak up. What is so important?"

As much as she tried, the words just couldn't make it out of her mouth. She stammered. She mumbled. She stuttered. The word just would not form. Finally, just as the major and the men were about to leave Sarah to her sputtering and pantomimes and continue their conversation, Hannah began honking the horn on her hard hat. The men raised their eyes from the plans and looked at Sarah with wonder and astonishment on their faces. This sort of broke the spell and Sarah was able at last to point across the river at the knot of Indians, and the word "*There!*" burst from her lips.

All eyes followed Sarah's pointing finger. Major Bradford saw the Indians, nodded, and told the little girl standing in front of him, "Yes, they have been there for quite a little while. They are probably just curious about all the activity that's going on. I expect we will hear from them in a couple of days. Nothing to worry about. Go back to your work. Everything is under control." He then returned to the plans that he held in his grasp.

Not sure that everything was safe but glad to be away from that stern face and those commanding eyes, Sarah turned to leave. As she did, Major Bradford looked up from the assembled group and said, "Oh, young lady. You have sharp eyes. You did the right thing. Keep up the good work. Thank you."

Wow! Maybe he's not such a bad man, thought Sarah. So with a smile on her face, the two time travelers continued their tour of the location. The site was beginning to resemble an honest to goodness camp. The tents were erected in straight rows, campfires had been lit, the farmland was being cleared, sections of the fort walls set in place, and in the center of it all was a big cook fire where a couple of the women were preparing the upcoming meal. Sarah thought this might be a good place to visit as the two girls were becoming hungry.

The fires were blazing, and the women were busy preparing the meal—cleaning, slicing, and chopping vegetables for the big black kettles that were beginning to boil. Off to one side was the ever-present coffeepot that was boiling the coffee grounds into a thick black, bitter syrup that would cling to a spoon like an ice cream bar clings to the wooden stick.

Sarah stood there stroking the furry bunny in her arms, wondering what she might be able to do to help the women assemble the meal large enough to feed sixty-five people. She was about to ask what she could do to help when Hannah said, "Those carrots and potatoes sure look good." *Honk. Honk.*

To this surprising statement, Sarah responded, "Hannah, you don't like carrots and potatoes. The only potatoes you eat are french fries."

"I don't know either, but they sure look good. I'm hungry! Ask that woman if we could have some to eat, okay?" *Honk.*

Approaching the woman with tentative steps and trepidation in her heart, she neared the cook. Just as she was about to ask for some carrots, the woman looked at Sarah who was standing beside her and said, "We are out of fresh meat. We need some meat for this stew. Go get the major. Maybe he will get us something for the stew."

With a little dread in her heart, Sarah headed back in the direction where she had last seen Major Bradford. She found him right where she had left him with the plans to the fort still in his hands. Pulling her shoulders back and lifting her chin, she approached the major. "Major, the woman making the stew said that there was no more fresh meat, and she wanted to know if you might be able to get some for her."

The major looked down at her and smiled. "Yes. I'll have a couple of the men go shoot some rabbits for the stew."

Honk. Honk. Honk. Honk. Honk. Honk. Honk. Honk. Honk. "That is unacceptable! I don't like what he just said! Sarah, get me out of here! This is not good! We need to find the chair and go home! I don't like stew!" *Honk. Honk. Honk. Honk.*

Doing an abrupt about-face, Sarah headed in the opposite direction from the camp. Looking for a quiet, isolated place, Sarah stuck Hannah inside her shirt to hide her from the hunters. She found an unoccupied area by the river a little distance from all the activities. "Okay, Hannah," said Sarah as she set the bunny on the rocky riverbank. "Get the cell phone and call for the chair. It's time we head back home."

The little bunny with the red hard hat produced the phone and in a hurry tapped in the number of the chair. The chair appeared almost before Hannah had a chance to hit the send button. As they situated themselves in the chair, Sarah noticed that the seat belt was unbroken and still tied together. "How did you fall out of the chair? It didn't break, and you didn't untie it. What happened?"

"I don't know, Sarah. I was just sitting there thinking about the dentist and how I wished that I was a rabbit so I could run away. Everything went black. When the lights came back on, I was a rabbit sitting on the side of the river."

"Oh, Hannah! That explains why you are an animal every time we go on an adventure. As we travel through time, you think of being an animal. When we get to our destination, you become that animal. Just be sure you don't think about an animal on our return trip back home. No telling what will happen."

As Sarah punched in the return address on the computer keyboard, Hannah said, "I just want to get out of this place. I want to go home. It is inpropiet to hunt rabbits when I'm a rabbit." Sarah tapped the enter key and away they went. The welcome sight of the plaid whale greeted them as always, and they knew they were soon going to be home.

They arrived back to the garage, and just as the lights reappeared, the door opened and their mom called the duo in for supper. Unfastening themselves from the time machine, they entered the house and pulled up their chairs at the kitchen table. There in front of them were steaming plates of all things…stew! The sisters looked at each other with wide eyes and they both said in unison, "This is not rabbit stew, is it?"

Their mother said, "Of course not. It's beef stew. Is something wrong with supper?"

Hannah said with relief in her voice, "No, everything is fine…just wondering." Still, she ate the vegetables and left the meat.

Leaving the dinner table, the girls sequestered themselves at the computer to see what they could find out about a Major Bradford and what they had just witnessed.

- Major Bradford led a detachment from Belle Fontaine, on the Missouri River, just outside St. Louis sometime around mid-September. The other half of the party met up with them near the mouth of the Ohio River. Major Bradford was not too happy because twenty-four of the new arrivals were too ill to work and needed medical attention. However, because of the slow progress down the river and the numerous stops to fix meals and repair the boats, many of them began to regain their health. When they reached their final destination, only four men were still unable to perform their duties.
- Accompanying the unit were two cannons and enough lead to outfit an army. Among the cadre

were six black troopers and four women. The black troopers had enlisted before the expedition and would serve for many years with the army. To keep up morale and to relieve the monotony of camp life, the expedition leader authorized the women to accompany the adventure. He recognized the importance of the fairer sex, and he would later encourage his officers and men to bring their wives to the post and the single men to marry the local women. These women went along to cook, clean, sew, and do the laundry. They were paid in money when it was available, paid in rations, or would barter for what they required. They would eventually marry, and they would become important personages in the local community.

- The trek was slow and onerous. Several reasons accounted for the time-consuming movement. The first excuse was the river current. The two keelboats were heading up river. That meant that they had to "pole" the boats against the river's current. If that wasn't enough trouble, the river had sandbars, falling banks, and floating trees that were constantly trying to inflict serious damage to the boats. Because of these unavoidable blockages and snags, the keelboats would need constant maintenance and repairs. This caused frequent stops, slowing their progress. Added to those problems were the sick members of the party. There had to be frequent stops to tend the sick and ailing.

- The party arrived at Arkansas Post, at the mouth of the Arkansas River, by the middle of October. At this time in its history, Arkansas had less than one thousand white settlers, most along the Arkansas River with the largest population probably collected around this French trading center. From there an advanced party of seven men was sent ahead under the command of Major Long. As this advance party continued against the rapid current in a skiff with oar lock and a small sail, they surveyed the river looking for just the right location to establish an outpost. They arrived at a promising site on December 1. Rowing ashore, they beached their small boat onto a rocky landing that was situated just below some commanding bluffs.

- Making a reconnaissance of the surrounding area, which was called Belle Pointe, Major Long decided that this junction of the rivers, the Arkansas and the Poteau, was the ideal location for the proposed fort. Belle Pointe was the location of an established French trading settlement. Leaving sketches for the fort and several men to await the arrival of Major Bradford and the rest of the detachment, Major Long took the rest of the advanced party and continued to survey more of the area to the south of Belle Point.

- During their trek up river, they passed several settlements and both white settlers and the local Indians wondered at the boats passing. On Christmas Day 1817, Major Bradford and his company of sixty-four troopers arrived at Belle Point. Camp was established, the keelboats were unloaded, meals prepared, and sentries placed at selected points. The ensuing days involved a lot of toil and labor. The land had to be cleared of trees and stumps, stones moved, stockade walls erected, and buildings established. Some of the troops would have begun clearing sections of land for the planting of crops. Here at this desolate outpost the fort would be self-sufficient for almost all their needs.

- Like most military outposts at that time, it began to draw settlers to the outlying areas. Before long, a thriving community would develop that would become a center of trade, commerce, and law and order for the land located to the west. While the major commerce was whiskey trading with the Indian population on the western side of the river, there was also a brisk trade with settlers heading into the lands west. This was even more brisk when gold was discovered in California, and it became a major stopping off place for people looking to strike it rich in the gold fields. This community would become a town and eventually a city. It would take its name from that given to the original army post, Fort Smith. Originally, Major Bradford named the outpost after the Commanding Officer of the Ninth Military Department, General Thomas A. Smith. It would be given the nickname of Little Gibraltar on the Arkansas.

- Fort Smith would be occupied by both the northern and southern armies during the Civil War. It was the hub of the Butterfield Overland Stage Line where the two routes met and continued on into California. With the establishment of the Federal Court system under the direction of Judge Parker in the old barracks building, it would acquire a less desirable name. It became known as Hell on the Border because of the cramped, stifling jail located in the basement of the building.

- Fort Smith had many trials and tribulations during its early years. The Fort was closed down many times and moved to the west, but the surrounding community would survive and become the second largest city in Arkansas. At one time it was said that there was no Sunday west of St. Louis and no God west of Fort Smith. Major Bradford is buried in the National Cemetery in Fort Smith not too far from where he established the original Fort Smith. Fort Smith has come a long way since then.

CHAPTER SEVENTEEN

Christmas! What a wonderful time of the year. A time of family, good eats, candy, sweets, and best of all, toys. To most children, Christmas is at the center of their universe. They wait impatiently for an entire year for that one single day.

The two girls anticipated about as much as they could stand before the holiday arrived. Thankfully for them, they were not disappointed in the least. They might not have gotten everything that was seen on TV, but it was close. Opening the presents consumed most of the morning. After a quick bite to eat, they went back to play with their new toys into the afternoon and evening. If the gift was especially coveted, it accompanied them to bed.

This behavior continued for a week or so; but over time, the pieces began to get lost, broken, or mixed with other toys. As the newness of the toys slowly began to wane, the girls began to look around for other worlds to conquer. In all the excitement and festivities of the holiday, the chair out in the cold garage was left unattended. But that was about to change.

Christmas vacation was rapidly coming to a close, and the sisters decided that it was time for at least one more adventure before school resumed. The major problem was the chair was sitting in the unheated garage. Not the most comfortable conditions for an adventure. The girls went to their mother and pleaded their case that the chair be brought into the house at least until warmer weather made its appearance. It took some beseeching of their mother with trembling, pouty lips and lost puppy-dog eyes fluttering, but they won their case. The chair was rescued from the cold garage and placed in the living room again.

Plans were discussed and made while the girls rummaged around their room looking for their time vortex uniforms that had been scattered about in different locations since their last visit in time. At last with the last of the uniforms located and donned, the room only slightly in disarray, the daring duo was ready for their last trip of the year.

They swaggered into the living room like they were members of the winning Super Bowl team. Nothing would stand in their way. They were ready for anything as they assembled themselves in the chair. As Sarah made her usual pre time travel inspections, Hannah began her checklist of equipment. Everything was in order except they hadn't yet decided where to go.

Deciding it really did not matter, they would let the chair decide; and Sarah just keyed in the number 1909. No reason. It just seemed like a nice number to her. Reaching down to hit the enter button, Hannah said, "Sarah, can I push the bunt-ton? Please?"

"Sure, Hannah. You do it."

With her hand poised above the keyboard, Hannah looked over at Molly, the family dog. "Ahhhh. Molly looks so cute. I wish she could go with us," said Hannah.

"There is no room in the chair. Molly will have to stay here."

"I know. But she looks so lonely," clucked Hannah as she pushed the enter button, and Sarah moved the lever out of park.

Slowly the chair began to move. The room began to shake and quiver. The waves of the carpet began to lap at the chair. Soon the furniture started to circle and jumble around the adventurers. Sarah said, "Mom is going to be upset with the mess we made of the living room."

"Not us Sarah, you!" responded Hannah.

"You helped make the mess. It's your fault too."

In short order, the furniture all blended into black-and-white stripes. The stripes morphed into a checkerboard. In the blink of an eye, the checkerboard appeared in the familiar form of the plaid whale. Just before the whale opened its gaping mouth to receive them into the jaws of darkness, Hannah giggled. "Sarah, I'm a…" Then all was quiet and dark.

CHAPTER EIGHTEEN

Sitting there in complete darkness and total silence, Sarah did not have to look or even feel. She knew she was alone in the chair. Where did Hannah go this time? What kind of trouble was she going to cause? Where were they?

Her hearing returned first. What she heard was the distant sound of a loud engine accompanied by a strange hiss. It was a familiar sound, but she was not quite able to recall what it was. As the darkness started to dwindle, her surroundings began to unfold. She was standing at the end of a rutted dirt street in a small town. Just in front of here was a painted sign that read, "Mill Town." The streets were unpaved. On each side of the road were a few stores that were open for business. Scattered about in the vicinity of the shops were houses where the townspeople lived. The houses and stores were clad with wood siding; some were painted in various colors and conditions. Large windows accompanied all of the buildings to allow as much sunlight in as possible. The large windows would also allow the cold blasts from the winter to enter the buildings. Most of the shops had covered wooden sidewalks or front stoops. She noticed that no cars or trucks were apparent in town. There were a lot of horses and horse-drawn carts or wagons located on the dusty road.

Any children who were present were mostly barefoot. The boys were attired in bibbed overalls. The girls were wearing dresses that came to about midcalf. They were playing much the same games that children have played ever since idea of children was first thought of. A few dogs intruded into the play and were barking and yelping in concert with the shrieks and yelling of the kids.

Standing beside the road, Sarah took in the surrounding landscape. The town was located in the middle of a wide prairie of golden grass that was tickled by the gentle breeze that emanated from the southwest. The picturesque landscape was surrounded by tree-covered mountains struggling to extend upward from the grass-covered earth. The sky was clear and blue, unblemished by smog or other pollutants. Dotting the azure sky were scattered cotton balls. The white billowy mists appeared to be resting on the broad shoulders of the tree-protected hills. It was as if they were taking a short rest before resuming their wanderings across the stratosphere. The crystal blue sky was punctuated by the large, dark-winged vultures that rode the thermal air currents that scaled the sides of the encircling hills. It was a pleasant town, and all the locals on the street seemed friendly and open to visitors.

Looking down the street, Sarah discovered the source of the loud engine and accompanied hissing. Down at the end of the street, not too far distant, sat a large black steam engine hooked in front of several passenger cars. Just on the other side of the snorting, chugging beast was a large building with several people milling around waiting for the train to depart. A sign fastened to the roof of the covered platform said "Midland Valley Railroad."

Sarah decided her best chance of locating her lost sister and finding out what town she might be in would be best accomplished at the train station. As she was heading in the direction of the station, she was passed by a small carriage pulled by a plodding mule that shuffled a wisp of dust with each step. The driver effortlessly held the reins in his large hands and only turned his right hand loose from control long enough to wave. On the side of the wagon were hand-painted letters that read "U.S. Mail."

Doing her best to avoid the noisy hissing engine and the men inspecting and working on it, Sarah stepped onto the covered platform. Immediately in front of her was a window and above the window was a sign that said "TICKETS." Just inside the window sat an elderly gentleman wearing dark green shades on his receding forehead and small wire-rimmed spectacles with smudged lenses riding his narrow nose. Covering his forearms were black pull-on sleeves that protected his white shirt from smudges and dust. Behind him, on the wall, hung a large calendar with the days marked out. The date on the calendar read 1909.

Continuing her visual tour of her surroundings, Sarah noticed several other people standing on the platform or perched on some benches reading papers or merely talking to others. Even with the warm weather, the men were all dressed in coats and ties. Many also wore vests with gold chains hanging from their pockets. Completing their attire were various hats of different descriptions and colors perched on their heads. They looked awfully hot to Sarah.

The ladies milling around the station looked just as warm as the men. They were attired in long skirts that ended just about their ankles and blouses that were fastened high on the neck. The dresses had long puffy sleeves. Their feet were encased in buttoned high-top shoes. Their hair was worn up and crowned with a hat, bonnet, or scarf. Each woman carried a purse. Several also had fans to help them keep cool and some even carried parasols even though there was not the least hint of rain. Sarah thought the umbrellas must have been to keep the sun off their fair complexions.

Something caught Sarah's eye. It was a flash of red nestled in a young girl's arms. It looked like a red hard hat. She couldn't be sure. Just as she was heading in the direction of the red flash, she heard, "All aboard. All aboard." The people waiting on the platform immediately began to board the cars, including the young girl holding the red flash. As the train began to pull away from the station, Sarah was left standing by herself. Not sure what to do, she made a dash for the last car on the train.

Barely able to catch the last car, she leapt aboard at the last second. Glancing over the passengers seated around the car, she was unable to locate the young lady with the red object. Moving down the aisle to the front of the car, she exited to enter the next car. However, Sarah found herself outside, surrounded by a landscape that passed her by at a rapid rate. The small platform was several feet from the rear exit of the next car. Looking down at the road bed as it rushed passed, she almost gave up. But she remembered what Grumpy had said: "If I can do it, you can do it." So gathering up her courage, and grasping on to any handhold that was available, she made the long step between the two cars.

She made it! Entering the door to the car, she immediately spotted the girl seated by herself. Walking down the aisle as best she could with the swaying and rocking of the train car, Sarah approached the girl. "Is anyone sitting here?" she asked, pointing to the seat across from the girl.

The girl looked up with her hazel eyes and said with a pleasant smile, "No. Nobody is sitting there, and I would enjoy some company."

As Sarah took her seat, the girl said, "Hello. My name is Eddra. What's yours?"

"My name is Sarah," Sarah said as she regarded the young lady. Although she was only five or six years older than Sarah, she sat with a gentile grace that seemed older than her years. A pleasant round face accompanied the smile that seemed genuine. Continuing her observation, Sarah noticed that on the seat beside her was a purse and in her lap was a red hard hat. Beneath the hat sat a small terrier puppy with pointed ears, wagging tail, and a pink tongue lolling out of the side of her mouth.

"This is my puppy, Daisy. I'm going to Fort Smith. How far are you going?" said Eddra.

"This train is going to Fort Smith, Arkansas?"

"Yes. Don't you know?"

"No," said Sarah. "I have lost my sister. I thought I saw her get on this train, so I got on at the last minute. Have you seen my sister?"

Honk. Honk. "Hi, Sarah. I'm over here. Do you see me?"

She did see Hannah, but all she could do was scowl at her because she did not want the young lady to think she was crazy by speaking to a dog.

Honk. Honk. "Sarah, don't you see me? I'm right over here."

Sarah tried her best to ignore her little sister. She looked at Eddra and asked, "Why are you going to Fort Smith?"

Before Eddra could answer, they both noticed a slender gentleman enter the front of the passenger car. He wore a white shirt buttoned up to the last button with a black bow tie cinched beneath his prominent Adam's apple. His coat and trousers were black as was his vest. The vest was accented by a heavy gold chain that connected to an official railroad pocket watch. On his head, perched in an official manner, was a black, flat-crowned cap with "Conductor" in white lettering. Clutched in his right hand was a shiny hole punch.

He approached the person sitting at the front of the car and said, "Ticket please." When he was handed the ticket, he proceeded to perforate the ticket with a series of holes. The chads fell like snowflakes to the floor of the car. He returned the ticket to the passenger and continued to the next seat where the performance was repeated.

By now Sarah was beginning to get antsy. She did not have a ticket or even any money to purchase one from the conductor. What was she going to do? She began to scan the interior for a convenient exit or someplace to hide. There just wasn't any. Where can you hide on a passenger coach traveling at fifty miles per hour? Hannah had gotten her in trouble again! Sarah began to fidget and squirm around in the seat. If Hannah had stayed with her and stayed off the train, this wouldn't be happening. What would they do to her? Arrest? Maybe they would only throw her off the train.

Eddra noticed Sarah's discomfort and asked, "What's the matter, Sarah? What's wrong?"

Sarah immediately became tongue-tied and even as she tried to answer, her tongue would not respond. "What's wrong? Don't you have a ticket?" asked the young lady.

"No. I thought I saw my lost sister get on the train and I just followed. I did not have time to buy a ticket. In fact, I don't even have any money to buy a ticket. What will they do to me?"

"Don't worry, Sarah. I'll take care of it. Leave it to me."

About this time, the conductor was standing beside their seat. "Tickets please. Oh, good morning, Miss Rooney. It sure is a nice day for a train ride, isn't it? Going into Fort Smith again?"

As the girls looked up at the gentleman, Eddra said, "Good morning, Mr. Pigg. Yes, we are going to the big city to see the bright lights." She gave Mr. Pigg a large grin and continued, "This is my friend Sarah. She is going with me to Fort Smith. Sarah, this is Mr. Pigg. He's the conductor on this train. What he says is the law, at least while on the train."

Mr. Pigg tipped his hat at Sarah and said with a pleasant smile, "Good morning, Miss Sarah. If you are a friend of Eddra's, then you are also a friend to me. I hope you young ladies have a nice stay in Fort Smith. Well, good morning, Miss Rooney, and you too, Miss Sarah. Maybe I will see you on your return." He then turned and proceeded down the aisle to litter the floor with more chads from the tickets in waiting hands.

To say Sarah was shocked would be an understatement. When she could form the words, she whispered to the young lady, "What happened? How did you do that? He didn't even ask for out tickets."

Eddra grinned and whispered back to Sarah, "You see, my father is the engineer of the train. I've known Frank, ah…Mr. Pigg for many years. Since my father works for Midland Valley, I get to ride to Fort Smith for free. I just told him were friends and traveling together. That's true, isn't it?"

With tears forming in her eyes and continuing down her cheeks, all she could do was say, "Oh yes, we are friends going to Fort Smith. I do not know how to thank you enough."

Honk. Honk. "See, Sarah, there was nothing to worry about. You worry too much."

"My pleasure," said Eddra. "Now what shall we talk about?"

They began to chat and natter away as only young girls are able to do. They jabbered on about school, family, pets, and "girl things." They became so engrossed in conversation that the time passed quickly, and before they realized it, Mr. Pigg came through the car announcing their arrival at the Fort Smith station.

Sarah said, "It's been nice to meet you, Eddra. Thank you so much for helping me. I think I had better get busy and find my lost sister. She is so much trouble." Looking at her sister in Eddra's arms, she continued, "Maybe she will be around the train station."

"My pleasure. I enjoyed the company."

Stepping down from the train car, Sarah looked around at her environs. She was standing on a covered platform attached to a long white stone and brick building. There were a lot more passengers and people waiting at this depot than the one they had just left. There were porters carrying bags. Others were pushing dollies with bags and packages and crates piled high. The ticket window had so many people lined up that Sarah was unable to notice what the man behind the bars looked like. Looking up, she noticed that carved on the gable of the building were the words "Midland Valley."

No sooner had Eddra stepped onto the platform than a young gentleman was standing beside her with a silly grin on his face. Sarah thought he looked a little familiar. He was about Eddra's age. He was tall and thin with an erect posture. His hair was parted on the right side and slicked back showing his large ears. He wore a white long-sleeve shirt buttoned all the way to his neck and his wrist, no tie or vest. Setting on his brown hair at a jaunty angle was a flat-brimmed straw hat, which he removed and said, "Good morning, Miss Rooney. You look awfully pretty today." Suddenly, Sarah knew who this young man reminded her of—her Grumpy.

"Hello, Walter. It is nice to see you. Have you been waiting long?"

"No, I just got here."

"Walter, I would like for you to meet Sarah. Sarah, this is Walter." Just about then, Daisy, the little terrier, with the red hard hat, leapt from Eddra's arms and launched into a yapping tirade as she took off around the corner of the building. "Oh, we need to catch Daisy before something happens. Sarah, you go around the building that way, and Walter and I will go this way. Maybe we get Daisy before she gets too far away." So Eddra and the young man took off following the direction that Daisy had taken. Sarah headed off in the opposite direction.

Before she could get to the far corner of the depot, she heard a *honk, honk, honk.* Sarah saw the black nose and pink tongue of the terrier poke around the side of the building. Hurrying to the edge of the white building, she caught up with her wayward sister. "We have to find someplace quiet so we can phone the chair and have it come pick us up," whispered Sarah. Pointing to the west, she continued, "Let's go over to that large building. It looks kind of deserted and overgrown with weeds."

Leading her sister to the brick building, she tried to stay under as much cover as she could. Well, leading was not the right word. The little terrier would trot ahead as if she was the queen of all she surveyed. When Daisy got so far ahead, she would stop, look back to make sure Sarah was still following, and then trot briskly back. *Honk. Honk. Honk. Honk.* "That means hurry up, Sarah, before somebody sees us."

While all this was going on, Sarah continuously said, "Don't get so far ahead. Someone might see you." Suddenly, Sarah came to a halt. "Hannah, look. This is Judge Parker's courthouse. Remember Granny and Grumpy would bring us here to look at the museum and to watch the fireworks on the Fourth of July."

Noticing several groups of people standing around the building, Sarah decided that they should find a more remote location. Looking around, she gathered up Hannah in her arms and circled the building, continuing heading west. *Honk. Honk.* "Eddra sure was nice, wasn't she? I will miss her."

"Yes she was. She sure helped us out. Now be quiet. We have to find some isolated place to meet the chair."

Honk. Honk. Honk. "That means okay."

Passing to the south of the building, they crossed two sets of railroad tracks into an overgrown, weed-en-shrouded patch of land overlooking the river. There among the tall weeds and thorns were several crude campsites and makeshift tents and hovels. Even though they saw no one around, Sarah did not like the looks of the isolated, men-acing place. Apparently, neither did Hannah because she began honking as she exclaimed, "Sarah, let's go back. This doesn't look very safe. Actually, Mom would not be very happy with us if the bad guys got us."

"I know, Hannah. Let's find somewhere else to call the chair." But when she turned around, she saw Eddra and Walter crossing the railroad tracks heading in their direction. Eddra was calling out Daisy's name, and Walter was trying to whistle up the pup. "Oh no! Here they come. We can't go back. They must not see us." Unmindful of the thorns, sticks, and waist-high weeds, they kept moving rapidly west until finally they descended a steep hill and arrived at the riverbank. They could go no farther.

They were standing on a rock-layered ledge just above the water level. They did note that imbedded into the black rock was a large iron ring. Not sure what it meant nor at the moment caring what it was for, Sarah decided that this was the time to dial up the chair and make a hasty retreat before something awful happened. She set Daisy (or was that Hannah?) on the rock-faced riverbank and said, "Okay, Hannah. Call the chair. We need to get out of here now."

Honk. Honk. "Sure," replied Hannah as she pulled out the phone and began to dial.

There was no puff of smoke or even a swirling of dust because they were standing on a rock bank that was continually swept clean by the lapping of the river's water. Suddenly, there it was. The chair in all of its junk-covered glory. Quickly fastening themselves into the chair, they prepared for time travel. Sarah keyed in the time, moved the lever out of park, hit the enter key, and away they went. Sitting there watching the adjacent countryside as it began to swirl and spin, Sarah suddenly said, "Hannah, I know where we are. This is Belle Pointe. This is where you were almost put into a stew pot. I knew it looked familiar." Those words were no sooner spoken then they entered the dark cavern of the hungry whale.

Arriving home, Sarah was glad to see that the living room was not all messed up and that Hannah was no longer a terrier puppy called Daisy. Curiosity about Milltown and the Midland Valley Railroad made the girls want to look into the past.

Locating their mother at the kitchen table, working on her scrapbooking, Sarah asked, "Mom, do you know anything about a Milltown or a Midland Valley Railroad?"

"Well, now let me think. I seem to remember Grumpy talking about them. I think Milltown was just the other side of Greenwood and we had some relatives from there. Midland Valley? I remember him talking about Midland Valley, but I can't really recall much about that. Why do you ask? What brought them up?"

"Oh, no reason. We just heard the names. We were curious. Weren't we, Hannah?"

"Oh, sure."

"Well, let's find out. Okay?"

The three of them adjourned into the living room, and Amber went to the bookcase and pulled down an old album. "This is an old genealogy book that Grumpy and his brothers worked on. Maybe this will help answer some questions."

Sitting on the couch with a girl on each side, they opened the book and began a trip through the family history. They started their excursion with Grumpy and his family. It wasn't a quick trip because they would become sidetracked by the many pictures and stories. When they got to Grumpy's father, both of the girls sat up and paid close attention. His father's name was Walter. Maybe this was it. However, there was no mention of Eddra or Mr. Pigg. The two girls relaxed a bit. That is until Amber turned the page.

There in front of them not only were the names Eddra and Walter but pictures as well. The pictures and the names matched. That was why the young man reminded her of Grumpy. They were Sarah and Hannah's great-great-great-grandparents. The girls became excited and very interested. Also, in one of the photos was Eddra with a little terrier, without a red hard hat, and written below was the inscription "Eddra with Daisy." Then Hannah noticed in another photo a steam engine with the crew standing in front and their names written on the bottom edge. In the middle was Hugh, the engineer, and beside him was the conductor, Frank Pigg. How wonderful. The three spent most of the day trolling through the old album.

Later, continuing their research, they found out the following information.

- Milltown is long gone. Regulated to its moment in history. What was once a pleasant rural community surrounded by coal mines is now merely listed as "a populated area" with a rural volunteer fire department.
- The Midland Valley Railroad was founded in 1903 to carry passengers and coal from the Greenwood, Arkansas, vicinity to Wichita, Kansas. It was a small railroad that used mostly already established rails for its service. The station in Milltown has long since gone the way of the dinosaurs. All that remains is the foundation and even then a person has to know where to look.

- The depot in Fort Smith was eventually abandoned and used for other purposes for many years. At one point, it was a feed and tackle store and was later loaned to the local Habitat for Humanity for storage and painting. Finally, it too was demolished to make way for "progress." The only remaining trace of the railroad, outside of fading pictures and failing memories, is the track that is being used at the Fort Smith Trolley Museum.

- The overgrown, weed-infested area that the girls passed through was the original Fort Smith. Abandoned by the military, it fell into disuse and was a temporary establishment, a "hobo jungle." It was referred to by the local residents as Coke Hill. That name did not come from the soft drinks. The name came from the use of coke, sterno, and other drugs and illegal commodities. It would not be a safe place for a couple of young girls to pass through.

- The ring imbedded into the rock bank by the river was used to tie up boats that landed at Belle Pointe. It can still be found near the water's edge where it has availed itself to any intrepid adventurers, traders, or wanderers for almost 200 years.

The girls learned a lot about their local history and were even privileged to have a close look at a small sampling of their own family history. And the two sisters are not finished yet. Sarah and Hannah have a lot more adventures to take in that wonderful, faithful old chair. As one adventure ends, another begins.

AFTERWORD

I would like to thank Rosie, my wife of quite a few wonderful, glorious, miserable years, for her encouragement, recommendations and criticisms of my work. She has made it a much more readable adventure. To David and Kara, thank you for humoring me when I just had to read a new chapter and asked for opinions. To my daughter, Amber, for her work on the book and for allowing me to enjoy my granddaughters, I thank you. To Sarah and Hannah for being a joy to be around and share in their inspirations and imaginations, thank you. Finally, to the editors and staff I thank you for your input and work to decipher my writings. Your effort has made this a more fluent and smooth flowing work.

Just a quick note about why the book was written. It is a follow up to *Welcome to My Chair*, but is a stand-alone read. The girls have visited each of the locations described in the book. All of these journeys are seen through the eyes of children. The history is fairly correct and accurate. There have been a few minor liberties and embellishments thrown in strictly for readability or some humor.

The time travel, of course, is purely fictional. I did try to tell the actions and interactions of the girls in a factual, if somewhat embellished, manner. Sarah and Hannah really are very well behaved children. The creation of the *Grumpy* was modeled after the experience the girls and I had building a twelve foot long submarine out of packing boxes and tape. It was one of the Christmas gifts that the girls received with great eagerness. The sub was rather elaborate with bulkheads, doors, periscopes, and hatchways. It sat in the living room for almost five months after Christmas. Thank you again, Rosie.

The bickering and fussing between the girls in the story was exaggerated but true. Generally younger siblings believe that they are placed on earth to aggravate their older brother or sister, and they usually know just what buttons to push and when to push them. I know this to be true because I was a middle child myself and had both an older and two younger brothers.

The room cleaning episode was another inflated event but retained an element of truth. Most parents, when frustrated because there is nothing for their children to do, make the mistake of telling them to "go clean your room." It is standard procedure for mothers, but placing two bored kids cleaning the same room can be challenging. It probably began with cave children being tasked with cleaning the mastodon bones out of the cave when they misbehaved. This admonishment is acquired over time and necessity by all new mothers and fathers. However, this technique is developed after they become parents, and it is too late to change plans and buy a puppy instead. This seemingly innocent statement can cause even more problems than it solves.

Now, one child cleaning his or her room is a study in how to force everything in the room into the closet and still manage to shut the door before everything cascades onto the floor. With two siblings cleaning the same room filled with their combined toys and other accessories, the previously mentioned study has taken on a special twist. It now requires a referee or maybe even a State Supreme Court Judge to oversee the effort and sort out which one is responsible for which mess. Not an easy task to say the least.

Sometimes the conflict is so bad that the room is divided down the middle with the admonishment to the other party, "This is my half of the room. You stay on your side. Keep your stuff on your side. I'll stay on my side." This will eventually be met with the response by the other party, "The door is on your side of the room. How do I get out?" This leads to another point of order as to who gets access to the closet and who doesn't. The argument continues with Mom stopping by the room several times to tell them to stop arguing and to get busy cleaning. Not that it does any good. This is one piece of parenting that does absolutely no good and only causes more finger pointing and recriminations. In time the room turns into a smaller version of the War Between the States without any actual bloodshed, in most cases.

Fortunately, unlike the actual war that lasted for four years, this divided room conflict only lasts a short while and soon harmony is restored and the kids are playing like always.

However, a clean room brings up another problem. When the room is cleaned, the kids can't find anything. But that is another section of the parenting class. Those parenting classes should be combined into a book and issued to adults to read before they become parents. That way they could make a sensible, educated decision whether to have children or just purchase some goldfish and have a life of their own.

So, just enjoy your children, your grandchildren and be glad that they are here for you. Sit back, or better yet, get involved and let them enjoy you as much as you do them. Appreciate their imagination and pretend, which is wonderful. Share their curiosity of the world and help them prepare for real life adventures. The time with your children is fleeting and only for the moment. Embrace your time with them. Watch them in their world as they grow and mature; it is very informative and enjoyable. It may help you to remember what it was like to be a child. You won't be sorry.

The book was interesting and enjoyable to write. I sincerely hope that the readers enjoy it as much.